ER RIVALS

SCARLET WILSON

MEDICAL ROMANCE

Recycling programs for this product may not exist in your area.

ISBN-13: 978-1-335-95285-1

ER Rivals

For questions and comments about the quality of this book, please contact us at CustomerService@Harlequin.com.

Harlequin Enterprises ULC
22 Adelaide St. West, 41st Floor
Toronto, Ontario M5H 4E3, Canada
www.Harlequin.com

HarperCollins Publishers
Macken House, 39/40 Mayor Street Upper,
Dublin 1, D01 C9W8, Ireland
www.HarperCollins.com

Printed in U.S.A.

1 2 3 4 5 6 7 8 9 10 HDC 29 28 27 26

Liam didn't normally clash with other doctors. He didn't often see them as rivals.

His original thoughts about Maggie had been that she was a doctor who had made a mistake. Now he realized that was wrong, he should probably apologize.

But apologies were the one thing that Liam knew he wasn't that good at.

He'd get to it, at some point.

Maggie pulled a list from her pocket. "I have a few things I wanted to go over with you."

He shifted in his seat and glanced around the staff room, where there were still a few people sitting. "Should we do this in my office?"

"Probably," she said, with the air of a person who didn't really care where she was having this conversation—she just knew she was going to have it.

He stood swiftly. "Let's go, then."

The walk to his office was short, and Maggie set the list down on the desk in front of her. She didn't wait to be invited to talk. "Look, I realize I'm new here, but there are a few things I need to bring up."

Dear Reader,

Even though I chose to set this story in Chicago, I still couldn't break with tradition of having a Scottish character in the story. Meet ER doc Maggie Sullivan, who is looking for her bad year to get a whole lot better. Unfortunately, her fellow Celt, Irishman Liam Kelly, isn't sure what to make of this challenging new doctor, and sparks fly with these ER rivals.

As with any good romance story, they both have hurdles to overcome before finally falling in love with each other. I hope you enjoy the story as much as I did writing it.

Love,

Scarlet

Scarlet Wilson wrote her first story aged eight and has never stopped. She's worked in the health service for more than thirty years, having trained as a nurse and a health visitor. Scarlet now works in public health and lives on the West Coast of Scotland with her fiancé and their two sons. Writing medical romances and contemporary romances is a dream come true for her.

Books by Scarlet Wilson

Harlequin Medical Romance

Christmas North and South

Melting Dr. Grumpy's Frozen Heart

Honolulu Medics

Hawaiian Kiss with the Brooding Doc

California Nurses

Nurse with a Billion Dollar Secret

Cinderella's Kiss with the ER Doc
Her Summer with the Brooding Vet
Nurse's Dubai Temptation

Harlequin Romance

Family Reunion in London

Christmas Surprise for Her Boss

Cinderella's Costa Rican Adventure
Slow Dance with the Italian
Mediterranean Dating Game

Visit the Author Profile page
at Harlequin.com for more titles.

This book has to be dedicated to my work bestie
and partner in crime for multiple years,
Kathleen Winter. Work won't be the same without you,
and I've treasured working with such a kind, fun and
dedicated nurse. Enjoy retirement—you deserve it!

CHAPTER ONE

THIS HAD HONESTLY been the worst month of Maggie Sullivan's life.

From the woman appearing on her doorstep in New York, and letting her know that Maggie's boyfriend of eighteen months was actually her husband. From the lease finishing on her apartment, and her new landlord backing out of their signed agreement with two days' notice. It seemed as though the world was sending her a message.

So, she finished packing boxes, looked online to find alternative emergency employment, then booked the first flight to Chicago. Her contract was for six months initially, with an option to continue if both parties agreed. She could live with that. She would use the time to decide if Chicago was a place she could call home or not.

The apartment she'd rented online had clearly used photos from years before. It was grubby and for some reason, even though the temperatures were good outside, inside it was cold and unwelcoming. There was a sort of smell about the place, which meant she didn't want to spend too much time there in case she ended up smelling like that too.

And that was how she'd ended up here, at Chicago Williams Memorial Hospital, an hour earlier than officially required. Another doctor who worked in the ER had been involved in an accident one month earlier, leading to a job opening.

From this point, things should have been great. Except, whilst Williams Memorial had up-to-date equipment, it was an old-style building that resembled a rabbit warren, meaning Maggie had got lost on the two occasions she'd left the ER—once to go to HR, and once to pick up her uniforms from the linen department.

The staff were friendly enough. The two charge nurses had shown her around the department, made sure she knew how to log on to the hospital systems, and that she'd been cleared to order tests and medicines.

After that? They'd pretty much left her to it. Not that she minded. Maggie had worked in emergency rooms across the world for the last seven years. Her parents in Scotland had died while she was in medical school, her dad from heart disease, and her mum from a lung disorder, and they'd always encouraged their girl to get out and see the world. Part of her jumping from country to country, and city to city, was to honour their memory. But the point was, she knew what she was doing in an ER. She'd been told the head of the department would meet her at some point, but after five hours, two pyrexial babies, a forty-five-year-old woman with a heart attack, a man with gastric pain, and two wrist fractures after some elderly women had collided at a walking group, Maggie was ready for a break.

'Dr Sullivan?' came the voice from the clerk at the front desk.

Maggie looked up; she was checking her pockets, trying to remember where she'd put her money. 'Yes?'

Lola, the clerk, had two police officers standing in front of the desk. 'These gentlemen are needing to be escorted to the morgue—to see the John Doe that came in overnight?'

Maggie frowned and racked her brain. This hadn't been on her shift, but she'd heard one of the charge nurses talk about the case earlier. Apparently, a young man with no ID had been found dead in one of the streets overnight.

'What do you need me to do?' she asked, finally locating her money in her scrub trousers. 'I was planning on going for a break.'

'Can you show them to the morgue first, please? We aren't allowed to send anyone down unescorted and I can't leave the desk.'

Her voice had almost a pleading tone and Maggie gave a reluctant smile. She got it. Not many people liked hanging out in the morgue.

She leaned across the desk and whispered to Lola, 'Where is it?'

Lola blinked then seemed to remember Maggie was new. She gestured behind her. 'Down the hall, down the stairs, take a right, another right and then a left.' She wrinkled her nose. 'I think…' She waved her hand. 'Never mind, you'll find it. Here's the code.' She handed Maggie a piece of paper with four digits written on it.

Maggie looked across at the cubicles. 'Can you tell someone I've gone for a break? I still haven't met the main guy yet, so if he appears, tell him I'm in the canteen.'

Lola nodded and Maggie smiled at the officers. 'Follow me,' she said as she started down the corridor, before shooting a glance over her shoulder at them. 'Don't suppose either of you have been down here before?'

Both shook their heads and she gave a sigh as she pushed open the door to the stairs. 'Well, let's just hope we don't all get lost.'

'Not from around here?' said the older man in a very matter-of-fact tone. It was a statement, rather than a question.

'Not that I know of,' she replied easily. She'd got this a lot since she'd moved to the US; her accent was a real giveaway. 'Decided it was time to spread my wings from Scotland.'

'East coast or west?' the guy queried.

'Got relatives there?' Just about every American she'd ever met had a relative somewhere back in the British Isles. Then she added, 'West…the *right* side of Scotland.'

The younger officer gave a laugh. 'That sounds like fighting talk.'

She swung open a door ahead. 'Oh, it definitely is. My great-grandmother committed the cardinal sin of marrying a west-coaster. She's still not been forgiven. Three generations on the west coast now. It seems the right place to me.'

She turned right, and then stopped, the first man nearly walking into the back of her.

The corridor ahead was pitch black. And the chill in the air was unnerving.

She shuddered and swallowed. 'It was definitely right that Lola said, wasn't it?'

The guy behind her shrugged. 'Sorry, wasn't paying attention.'

'Right,' she said, her stomach giving a low growl. She really needed to eat something.

She took a breath and moved a few steps forward, the lights flickering on above her. She glanced upwards. 'Must be those energy-efficient lights. I'm assuming we'll be fine.'

The younger man looked from side to side and gave a nervous laugh. 'Here's hoping we're not about to take part in a horror movie.'

Maggie's skin prickled in discomfort. A few

minutes later, it was clear they were going the wrong way. Lola's directions were not entirely correct. What was worse was the fact that literally no one was around.

As they turned back in one of the corridors for the second time, Maggie put her hands on her hips and shouted, 'Hello, anyone here?' There was not a single sign in the area they were in. At least the rest of the hospital had signposts. She muttered this under her breath and the older officer gave a low reply.

'Guess they're not expecting any patients down here. Well, live ones, anyway.'

The lights had started to go out behind them again, and it was unnerving her. She hated feeling like that; it wasn't normal for her.

Eventually she turned another corner and saw a door that did actually have a sign. The word 'Mortuary' was kind of battered in appearance. She almost let out a sigh of relief.

She pulled the card from her pocket and punched in the code that Lola had given her, taking a step into the room and letting the lights go on around them.

There was no mortuary technician in attendance, but there was a chart on the wall with the names of the residents of the mortuary chambers. Maggie scanned the list, thankful there was only one apparent John Doe showing.

She slid the chart back into the wall. 'It's

drawer seven,' she said, walking over to the drawer and putting her hand on the chilly handle.

This still struck her as so strange. Why was there no one around? It wasn't late. It was barely mid-afternoon. Was the morgue always left with no staff?

She licked her lips and glanced at the officers, who were clearly just as uncomfortable as she was. This was ridiculous. Unfortunately, in Maggie's line of work, there had been plenty of opportunities to deal with dead bodies. It wasn't as difficult as some people might have thought. She'd told herself early on to just imagine that everyone was sleeping. And, for the most part, that had stood her in good stead.

She breathed in and pulled. The door slid open smoothly, but with a loud rattle. The body was covered in a white sheet.

'Did you say he had identifying features?' Maggie asked, wondering if she would have to uncover the whole body or only part of it.

'Potentially, two tattoos,' said the older man. 'A bird on the right forearm, and a US marine tattoo on the left outer bicep.'

Her hand paused in mid-air. 'This man was a marine?'

The man shrugged but still looked serious. 'Could be.'

There was an echo down the corridor and for a second Maggie thought she heard a voice. She paused for a second, then lifted the side of the sheet covering the left bicep. There was no obvious tattoo.

'I think we might have the wrong guy,' she started to say, before everything changed.

It was in literally the blink of an eye.

The arm of the so-called corpse lifted straight up, followed by the man sitting upright and the sheet falling from his face.

Maggie let out a scream and jumped back. She couldn't help it. Both officers did their own version, just as an unknown man wearing scrubs burst through the door.

'What the…?' he said loudly.

The corpse blinked and shuddered. The unknown man had covered the area in long strides, touching the corpse's arm and clearly taking a radial pulse. Maggie still hadn't moved. She couldn't actually breathe right now.

'Sir, are you okay?' the man in scrubs asked. His head whipped to the officers and then to Maggie. 'Does one of you want to explain what the hell is happening down here?'

Maggie was pretty sure she could hear her own pulse echoing in her ears. Her body swayed and she reached out both hands. Not eating before coming to work today clearly hadn't been a good idea. One of the men caught her from behind, and she steadied herself, and contemplated throwing up on the floor.

The corpse started speaking. 'Sorry, sorry.'

'What are you sorry for?' asked the man in scrubs. 'I'm Dr Kelly. We should be apologising to you. Clearly,' his gaze fixed very angrily on Maggie, 'you should never have been brought down here.' Something in her brain pinged. The recognition of his thick Irish accent.

The corpse tried to swing his legs off the drawer but then clearly realised he was naked and clutched his sheet around him. 'Miles Cooper,' he said, giving his head a shake. 'I have narcolepsy with cataplexy.'

Dr Kelly sucked in a breath. 'Paralytic sleep with imperceptible vital signs. So, you knew what was happening the whole time?'

Miles nodded.

'You must have been terrified.' Maggie had finally found her voice. She could tell Dr Kelly was still angry—his shoulders were tense and the tone of his voice dripped with fury. Somehow it seemed as if some of this fury was being directed at her. And if his name was anything to go by, this was likely Liam Kelly—the head of the department who'd been supposed to meet her.

Great first day.

'This isn't the only time it's happened,' said Miles, a hint of a smile appearing on his face.

Okay, so now Maggie was getting her breathing and heart rate back to normal. Was this guy for real? 'This has happened before?' she asked incredulously, wondering if she was still in her bed in that strangely cold apartment and this was just part of a weird dream.

Colour was starting to seep into his cheeks now. He was beginning to resemble someone from the land of the living.

But before she even got a chance to get a reply, Dr Kelly shot words over his shoulder to her, 'Well, I'd hate to think you'd done this before,' in a biting response.

Liam Kelly's day had gone from bad to worse.

He'd been late to work. Anyone who knew him knew that Liam was late for nothing. But there had been an accident on the motorway and, of course, he'd stopped to assist.

He'd known he was supposed to meet a new doctor today—one he hadn't interviewed or chosen, but he was trying to let that go.

Motsi Gatwa had left at short notice after being involved in an accident. He'd been astonished when someone had apparently applied on the first day the hospital had advertised the post. Her checks had been rushed and she'd been due to start today.

Liam had been sceptical. All the good doctors had posts. While there could be exceptional circumstances, his view was that doctors who were available at short notice were generally available for a reason—and that usually wasn't a good one.

He hadn't even had time to do some quiet checks on Maggie Sullivan and it was clear he should have.

'I've seen a lot of things in my years as a doctor,' he said, 'but a corpse waking up is not one of them.'

Miles grinned at him and rubbed his arms. 'Glad I'm your first. But it's kind of cold in here. What's the chance of some clothes?'

Maggie Sullivan moved. She pulled out a bag underneath the drawer which clearly contained Miles's belongings and dumped them next to him. Not only had she declared him dead, but she now didn't have the good grace to treat her patient with respect.

She picked up a pair of dirty, sodden jeans. 'What did you do?'

Miles stared in surprise at his wet, dirty clothes. 'I have no idea.' He looked towards the officers. 'Where did you guys find me?'

The older man cleared his throat. 'It wasn't us, but you were found near one of the ferry stops on the Illinois river.'

Miles looked at his clothes. 'Was I in the river?'

The officer shrugged. 'Apparently you were cold and wet, and when they brought you here they said you were dead. You had no ID.'

'Where is here?' asked Miles.

Liam answered him. 'Chicago Williams Memorial Hospital. Okay, I'm going to get you a wheelchair and take you back up to the ER to check you over.'

Miles looked a bit wary, and he couldn't blame the guy. Maggie stepped forward. Her Scottish accent was thick and she put her hand on Miles's shoulder. 'You said this had happened before?'

He blinked and nodded. 'Twice before.'

'And what? You didn't think to get an alert bracelet?'

She was annoyed. At least she had some spirit. She pushed a strand of her blonde hair behind her ear. She was pretty too. But he couldn't think about that. Because Maggie Sullivan had already committed a cardinal sin in his book. She'd made a mistake at work, and that was a line in the sand for Liam.

Miles gave her a nonchalant glance. 'And what? Spoil the surprise for people?'

'I guess you'll be the one getting the surprise if the coroner actually starts cutting,' she snapped.

'Enough!' Liam glared at her. It was time to put this Scottish firecracker back in her box. 'Get me a wheelchair.'

Her eyes were blazing and she looked around the mortuary, realising there was no wheelchair in sight. After a few seconds, she stalked out of the door.

Liam turned to the officers. 'Was Miles the man you were sent to identify?'

They both nodded but then the older man

shook his head. 'He's not who we suspected him to be. Just as well you don't have amnesia,' he said to Miles. 'But you clearly don't have your wallet either. Do you know your address?'

Miles nodded. 'Don't worry, I know who I am and where I live. I can call someone to come and get me.'

'Only once you've been checked over again,' said Liam.

The door banged open and Maggie appeared with a wheelchair. 'Sorry,' her smile was definitely on the sarcastic side. 'There don't seem to be any accessible door openers down here.'

She helped Miles into the wheelchair; she'd also managed to acquire a theatre gown and blanket from somewhere and she arranged them around him.

Liam finished with the officers, then, pushing Miles in the chair, made his way back along the corridors to the lifts. Maggie walked alongside, not talking. He wasn't at all sure what to make of her.

He waited until they exited the lift and he pushed Miles into one of the cubicles in the ER. 'Can you get me the original notes, please?' he asked.

She disappeared for a few moments and came back clutching a tablet. Since Miles's true identity hadn't been known when he was admitted, he was known as John Doe 107. Liam didn't really want to think about how many actual patients had appeared in this ER over the years with no identity.

He did some standard checks on Miles. Heart rate and blood pressure were normal; oxygen saturation was in the normal range too. For a man who'd had literally no sign of life at some point today, he seemed remarkably fine.

'Are you seeing anyone about your narcolepsy and cataplexy?' he asked.

'I see a neurologist, Dr Javid.'

'And do you have a treatment plan?'

Miles gave a weak smile. 'Try not to let it happen somewhere dangerous?'

There was a noise beside him, and Liam could see Maggie step up next to him.

'Do you get any kind of warning before an attack?'

Miles gave a half-shrug. 'I can feel very tired. And have some slurring when I speak or facial weakness. Really, it just comes on very suddenly.' He held up both hands. 'But I'm not going to stop living my life. I just have to deal with it.'

Maggie gave him a stern look. 'I think you should consider spoiling the surprise.'

He wrinkled his nose. 'What do you mean?'

'What she means,' Liam cut in, 'is that your condition is dangerous. You've ended up in a hospital morgue more than once. What happens if we hadn't come down to the morgue today? You might not realise it, but those drawers don't open from the inside. You could have been in there overnight, and been at risk of dying from hypothermia.'

Miles didn't reply.

Maggie kept going. 'Do you have a driver's licence right now?'

Miles pulled a face. 'I've never had an episode in the car.'

Liam felt himself stiffen. This guy didn't only have a wave of ambivalence about his own life, but also for other people's.

'I'm going to recommend that your driving licence is suspended until you have more investigations.' He glanced down at the tablet in front of him.

'You can't do that!' exclaimed Miles.

Liam looked back up, keeping very calm. 'Oh, I can, and I will.'

'Then I'll sue. I'll sue this hospital for putting me in a morgue when I wasn't dead.'

'And our lawyers will want to know why—when you know you have these conditions—you don't see fit to wear a warning bracelet.'

'I shouldn't need to, because a doctor should know if someone is dead or not.'

'I agree,' said Liam, deliberately not casting his eyes towards Maggie. 'But you've said yourself this has happened before.'

'It has,' said Miles quickly.

Liam took a breath. 'And when it happens, when you feel yourself lose control and sensation in your muscles—you're still aware, aren't you?'

Miles nodded but didn't speak. Liam knew he had to try a different tack with this guy.

Liam licked his lips. 'And I imagine that must be terrifying. Knowing what's happening around you, but not being able to attract any attention.'

Miles gave a little shudder. Liam was beginning to get it. This guy put on a front. And whilst initially it might seem jarring, there was much more to it.

Liam spoke carefully. 'I can't imagine how it must be getting zipped into a body bag, or having a sheet placed over your head, or hearing the sound of the drawer closing.'

'I can't move, not even blink,' said Miles in a disjointed voice, 'not even when my brain is screaming at me and willing me to move. Move anything, to show a sign that I'm still in there.'

Liam gave a slow nod. 'Has your neurologist suggested some counselling?'

He could sense Maggie drawing a little closer, listening to every word. He'd tried to blot her out, and just focus on the patient, but as she moved into his line of sight he could see the compassion on her face. He could smell her light amber scent.

Liam moved, perching next to Miles on the ER trolley. 'So, if you're telling me you can't move, even if you wanted to, can you imagine what would happen if you were behind the wheel of a car?'

Miles didn't speak.

Liam continued. 'Can you look me in the eye and tell me, categorically, that if you had some warning, you would be able to pull over safely to the side of the road?'

Miles looked anywhere but at Liam.

Maggie stepped forward and put her hand on Miles's arm. 'It's time to look after yourself, and others around you. You need to get some kind of medic alert. A bracelet. Something around your neck. Anything that will alert people around you that you have a particular condition.' She gave a shudder. 'As Dr Kelly said, if those cops hadn't come to identify you, you might have been down there for hours—maybe even overnight.'

Miles took a tight breath. It was clear there was much he still had to deal with. 'I'll think about it,' he said gruffly.

Liam gave a nod. 'We'll run another few tests then hopefully I'll be able to clear you to go home. You said there was someone you can call?'

Miles nodded.

'And would you like something to eat and drink meantime?'

As if in response, Maggie's stomach gave a little growl and her hand flew to cover it as colour rushed into her cheeks.

Miles gave a little laugh. 'Yes, please,' he said.

'Okay, then.' Liam ducked out behind the curtain. 'Dr Sullivan, with me, please.'

He moved down the corridor and stopped one of the orderlies. 'Can you get a sandwich and something to drink for the guy in curtain twelve, please? He just woke up in the morgue, so let's not have him fainting when he leaves.'

The orderly gave a laugh and shook his head as if he heard this kind of stuff every day. 'No probs, Liam,' he said with a wave of his hand.

Maggie started to talk as they continued down the corridor. 'Sorry about that,' she said quickly. 'I was just about to go for a break when I was asked to take the police officers down to the morgue.'

Liam opened the door to an office and led her inside, firmly closing it behind her and walking around to the other side of the desk.

'Take a seat, Dr Sullivan.'

'Maggie,' she said quickly. 'Call me Maggie.'

He took a breath and waited for her to sit opposite him. Head on, he got the full effect. He'd already clocked the fact that Maggie Sullivan was an attractive lady. But sitting opposite her, in bright lights like these, meant there was nothing he could miss. From her bright green eyes, to her blonde mid-length hair, currently caught in a ponytail, to the perfect skin, a few scattered freckles across her nose, and the easily symmetrical features and straight teeth.

Really, she could be on a movie poster rather than sitting across from him in a Chicago ER.

'Maggie,' he said steadily, 'do you think you can explain to me why a patient was declared dead, and taken to the morgue, when he was actually alive?'

Liam was trying hard to keep his temper in check. He'd seen mistakes before. Just about every doctor he'd ever known had made mistakes along the way. In fact, it was the whole reason he'd got into the profession. Twenty years earlier, someone had made a mistake which had cost his brother his life. Liam had vowed to spend his life making sure that didn't happen again. But here, in his department, it had just happened in a spectacular way.

He watched as she straightened in her chair. 'Excuse me?'

The accent was strong. If he wasn't familiar with Scottish accents he might not have heard her clearly.

'Why would I excuse you?' was his blunt reply.

Her green eyes flashed. 'Do you want to take a few steps back, and introduce yourself properly to me?' she shot in return, sitting back in her chair as if she was making herself comfortable.

'Liam Kelly, Head of Department—you report to me.' The words were practically a growl.

Her eyebrows rose. 'Oh, the Liam Kelly who was supposed to meet me on arrival to show me around the department, the hospital and introduce me to the staff?' She pulled out her phone from her scrubs pocket. 'You're five hours late.'

He took a second. She'd made a mistake—one that could have proved fatal—and didn't seem to be taking responsibility for it. Not only that, but she was also being disrespectful and insolent at their first real meeting.

'You won't be employed here much longer if this is your attitude.'

'What exactly do you think you can sack me for, Dr Kelly? I got here an hour early, collected my ID and scrubs and started seeing patients straight away. Feel free to check all my charts. I'm no novice. I've worked in ERs for seven years. I know what I'm doing.' She counted off on her fingers. 'Two pyrexial babies, one with chickenpox, one with a virus. A forty-five-year-old female with a tombstone MI. A man with epigastric pain—likely due to the all-you-can-eat breakfast buffet across the street—and two elderly ladies who collided at a walking group and now having matching Colles fractures, one with a pink cast and one with a lilac cast.'

She crossed her legs and stared angrily at him. 'Check my charts. I'll wait.'

On any other day he might have stopped to take a look. A tombstone MI had a high mortality rate—the lady was lucky it had been spotted quickly. But a low-grade rage was already building inside him.

'I will,' he snapped, 'after you explain to me why you declared someone dead and sent them to the morgue.'

'I didn't,' she said. 'I only escorted the police down to identify the body.'

He blinked and checked the tablet in front of him. When he'd come on duty he'd asked where Maggie was. One of his nurses had told him that she'd gone down to the morgue with the police to help identify a body from earlier. As he replayed that sentence, he realised the nurse hadn't actually specified *when* the man had been declared dead. It was normal in this set of circumstances that if the doctor was still on duty when the police came, that they would accompany the police to the morgue to answer any additional questions if necessary. As he glanced at the tablet, he could see Miles was declared dead at five thirty a.m. He recognised the name of the doctor. Maggie's shift started at seven. It was before she started.

He swallowed and met her gaze.

'Now we've got that sorted,' she said, standing up and staring down at him, 'it's good to know what kind of person I'm working with. Heaven help the poor doctor that declared Miles dead. I can only imagine the kind of reception you're going to give them. As for me…' She'd actually folded her arms now. Maggie wasn't the tallest.

Probably only around five feet five. But, from here, sitting in a chair opposite, she looked like quite a formidable force. 'Since you don't seem to know how to organise breaks for your staff, and I've been here for over six hours now, I'm going to go and get something to eat.' She fixed a smile on her face. 'That should give you plenty of time to try to pick holes in my charts while I'm gone.'

She stood up then paused at the door. 'Dr Kelly,' she said in a low voice, 'don't treat me like a fool,' and she turned on her heel and walked out of the door.

Liam sat back in his chair, stunned.

He grabbed the tablet and checked the details again. Yep. It was another doctor who had declared Miles dead and sent him down to the morgue. But he could also see the name of one of his senior nursing staff on the chart. He would never have chalked a mistake like this down to them.

He shook his head. Both of these staff members would be called into formal meetings. Something like this was serious—and had to be treated that way.

But something else was bothering him. Not only had he got off on the wrong foot with his new doctor, but it also seemed as if she might be trouble.

He pulled up the HR file to check her job history and her references. He recognised a few of the hospital names. But he didn't know anyone that worked there.

Her references were good. But none of those names were familiar either.

He sat back again and thought hard. Why was she available at such short notice? Doctors applied for jobs and programmes months in advance. When they'd advertised the job, they weren't even sure if anyone with the right skill set would be available to apply.

She'd been working somewhere else—he checked again: New York. She must have left them at short notice; that couldn't have gone down well.

Now he leaned back and breathed. Sure, she had a résumé of ERs that corresponded with what she said—seven years' experience. And her references were good. But somehow he felt as if something was missing.

Liam Kelly didn't like mysteries. He wanted to know who he was working with, and just how good they were. The patients that came into Chicago Williams Memorial's ER were his responsibility and he would ultimately answer for their care.

So he bent forward, and picked up the phone.

CHAPTER TWO

MAGGIE ALWAYS TRIED to control her fiery temper at work. But yesterday had been a complete blow-out.

She'd actually been enjoying her first few hours at the new hospital, right up until Liam Kelly had crossed her path. What an arrogant, egotistical brat of a man!

She could think of a few choice Scottish words to describe him—but they were all words her long-deceased granny would have slapped the back of her head for if she'd heard her say them.

She was still trying to ignore the fact that for a least a millisecond—when he'd first burst through the doors of the morgue—she'd been struck by how handsome he was. But as soon as he'd opened his mouth and started his tirade, those thoughts had been pushed back into the small, dark box they belonged in.

But for some reason his tall, lithe frame, sandy-coloured hair and blue eyes were stuck in her head. Along with his Irish accent, which was an absolute killer. She knew friends of hers would pay money to listen to a voice like that.

But that didn't mean anything. The guy still needed a kick up the backside.

She was furious at being accused of a mistake that wasn't hers. What made her even *more* furious was his reaction. Doctors made mistakes. They were human. And how you treated a person after a mistake at work was extremely important.

Mistakes had consequences. But there was always learning to be done. Pathways and protocols that could be improved to help prevent mistakes being made in future. Raising awareness of particular issues or conditions could always improve knowledge and learning.

Early in her career she'd gone to a risk seminar during which the lecturer had used a real-life example: a patient had a condition that most doctors weren't familiar with, so were unfamiliar with treatment doses. The regular pharmacist at the hospital was on their break when the patient's pre-made medicines arrived. A nurse, who knew the patient, hung their IV meds, assuming all the normal checks had been done. When the patient became unwell, no one immediately thought to check the medicines because the patient had been given them many times before.

The outcome was horrendous. The patient died due to an overdose of what should have been safe medicines.

The lecturer had described the incident as a piece of Swiss cheese, where all the holes lined up at one point. Lots of points where someone could have stopped and double-checked things. Opportunities missed, resulting in fatal consequences. Maggie had never forgotten that scenario, and knew that extra checks that might even annoy others were worth it.

Could she work in an environment where it seemed that blame could be laid at someone's door? Where it was possible that supportive conversations and opportunities for learning weren't embraced?

She shuddered as she swung her legs out of bed and wrinkled her nose at the smell. Fousty. A Scottish word she could use. This place definitely had an old, mouldy odour around it. She half expected to see a piece of cheese sitting in the middle of the floor, or obvious dampness on the walls—which she hadn't discovered as yet. But the smell was definitely there.

She sighed and flung open her case to find some clothes for the journey into work. She also needed to find a local coffee shop and somewhere she could pick up some groceries. With the timing of everything, she hadn't really given herself a chance to familiarise herself with the neighbourhood.

She'd left in such a hurry after the meeting with her boyfriend's wife. She still couldn't wrap her head around it. There must have been signs. She'd dated him for eighteen months. How could she not have noticed he had a wife hidden away somewhere?

Her phone buzzed and she picked it up. Shona. A friend from New York.

Well, things have kicked off here. Ryan came to the department to find out. He is MAD.

Her fingers flew quickly.

What's he got to be mad about? He's the one with a wife.

He seems to think you're responsible and met his wife to tell her all about the two of you.

Anger surged under her skin. How dared he blame her for his own mess? But she took a breath and typed slowly.

I don't really care what he says, or what he believes anymore. At least I'm not there to be lied to, or manipulated. Just make sure he doesn't find out where I've gone, and don't give him my new number.

Of course not! came the quick reply. I've got your back x

Maggie gave a sigh. She'd moved here to get away. To start a new life. Make new friends. Look for new opportunities. Liam Kelly might be her boss. But that was all he was.

And Maggie had no problem telling him exactly what she thought.

She tossed her hair back and headed to the shower. She'd deal with the smell in here later.

The calls had been a bit odd. First of all, the person he was talking to wanted to verify who he was. They'd insisted on being given a telephone number, and then called the hospital's HR team before they would give any information out.

They verified that Maggie had worked for them, been an excellent doctor, that they had no concerns about her. When Liam had tried to press for a little more information he'd hit a brick wall.

He'd stayed late last night to talk to the doctor on the night shift that had certified Miles as being dead.

It had been an interesting conversation. The doctor had been shocked, then bewildered that something like that could happen. He'd heard of both conditions but never come across a patient affected by both at the same time. Liam had done what he always did when there was a mistake at work: talked the person responsible through it, asked some pertinent questions that he hoped would make the doctor think, then asked him to write it up, along with any recommendations that could prevent something similar happening in future.

He'd agreed to meet with the doctor again in a few weeks' time to go over the notes and see if there was anything that the department could learn from the incident.

People found Liam Kelly pedantic, and he didn't care. Not even a little.

But that didn't help with his latest recruit.

There was something about Maggie Sullivan that he couldn't quite put his finger on. Ignoring the fact she was extremely attractive, and according to herself and others a 'good' doctor, he'd found her attitude last night…interesting.

There were other words starting with an *i* he could use instead. Insubordinate. Irritating. Or he could move through other letters of the alphabet. Abrupt. Brusque. Challenging. Defiant.

But he was trying hard not to. Because he had to work with this woman for the next six months. He needed to be able to trust that she would do a good job, and know that she could handle the stress of working in an ER.

If she was going to challenge him at every point, this could be an uncomfortable experience for them both. He didn't even want to admit that he actually had gone back and checked her charts. At the end of the day, he should have been there to meet her for her first shift. If she'd made mistakes on that shift, he was entirely responsible, so checking her charts had seemed like a reasonable thing to do.

He hadn't found any mistakes. She'd diagnosed the forty-five-year-old woman with the tombstone MI remarkably quickly—particularly when she'd come in with indigestion. There had been none of the usual MI symptoms and the woman was a fitness instructor with an in-range BMI. For most doctors, MI wouldn't have jumped out as a first call.

Liam would have to take the next few shifts to determine what he actually thought of her. There was a noise at his feet and he looked down to see Barclay, his rescue beagle, looking at him as though he was a pure inconvenience.

Liam sighed and walked over to the treat cupboard to pull one out, careful how he positioned his hand. Barclay was a biter. When he'd asked at the rescue centre which dog they'd had trouble rehoming, there had been some eyerolling and a few fingers pointed to Barclay.

Liam didn't know the circumstances around Barclay's rescue, but he'd learned enough about beagles to know that some owners considered them untrainable, they were entirely scent-driven, focused on food, and a little bit lazy. Liam had quickly accepted the fact he would never be the boss of this dog, and only hoped that daycare wouldn't throw him out.

He fitted the harness over Barclay and pulled on his jacket for work. The walk was only forty minutes and the daycare centre was on the way, so he was there with enough time to spare to head to the canteen for some food.

As he headed over to a table filled with ER staff, he realised that Maggie was sitting at the end. She'd remarked she hadn't had a break yesterday. Maybe she'd decided to stock up before starting today?

He said hello to the surrounding staff as he sat down and started on his chicken pie. 'We're down two surgical fellows,' said a voice in his ear.

He turned. One of the senior gastric surgeons looked decidedly unhappy. 'What's happened?' he asked.

The guy rolled his eyes. 'Food poisoning. They've actually both been admitted. So, if you're looking for a consult today, it could take a while.'

'Having to do your own grunt work?' Liam said easily, because this surgeon was renowned for being decidedly lazy.

The man scowled at him.

'I'll keep that in mind if we have to call,' he said, spearing a bit of chicken and watching the surgeon stalk off.

He heard a murmur at the bottom of the table about 'making friends' and glanced up to see Maggie looking at him. Her green eyes caught his and she gave a little shake of her head before tackling her own plate of food.

His skin prickled. Was she deliberately trying to annoy him and pick fault? Because the ER had to be a team. He didn't need anyone who wanted to cause animosity in his team.

She hadn't changed into her scrubs yet, and was wearing a pink shirt. It complemented her colouring but he wasn't supposed to notice that, so he looked quickly away.

The chat around the table was casual. A few new patients were mentioned, and a few cases from the day before. He wondered if they'd already finished the chat about the patient who'd been declared dead before he'd got there.

As they finished their meals and stood to leave, he found Maggie at his elbow. 'I'll give you the proper tour of the department today,' he said quickly.

She gave a shrug as she slid her tray onto the rotating rack. 'Not sure I need one now,' she said in a low voice.

'Well, let's just do everything properly,' he replied, his tone sharper than he intended.

'Fine,' was the one-word response.

She disappeared and by the time he saw her again in the ER there was a stream of ambulances at the door.

Liam moved to triage. First patient was a seizing toddler. That one went straight to Paediatric

Resus. Next was an older man with a broken hip who'd been lying outside and was also hypothermic. It wasn't particularly cold in Chicago at this time of year, but the elderly were always more prone to hypothermia. After that was a teenager who'd been found unconscious in her sorority house.

He followed her into the resus room, where Maggie had started work on the other side of the curtain. 'How's that toddler?' he shouted through to her as he connected his teenager up to the medical equipment.

'Just getting a line in for some meds,' she shouted back.

He paused, just for a second; getting a line into a seizing toddler would be hard for anyone, but he didn't want to presume. 'Shout if you need a hand.'

He focused on the teenager in front of him. 'What's the story?' he asked the paramedic.

'Last seen by her friends a day and a half ago. Had been to a party. Said she didn't feel great and came down for some water and paracetamol. When they checked on her today, they couldn't wake her up.'

'Obs?'

The paramedic rattled them off her. Her temperature was raised and her GCS was 10.

'Anyone with her?'

The woman shook her head. 'University is contacting her next of kin.'

'None of her roommates came along?'

'Sorry, no.'

The nurse next to him gave him the glance. The one that spoke a thousand words.

'Think they might have been doing drugs?'

He nodded, and rhymed off a range of blood tests for the patient. But her altered conscious state was giving him the most concern. 'She has a temperature. Do we know her vaccination status?'

One of the admin staff had been clerking her in on a nearby tablet. 'If she's a local I can probably get it; if she's from out of state, not likely. The university just gave basic details and next of kin. No doctor listed.'

Liam lifted her eyelids and checked her pupils. 'Sluggish, and we have no real medical history for her. What if this isn't drugs?'

'Don't all the universities insist students are vaccinated?'

'Some do,' said Liam. 'But I'd hate to make any assumptions without facts.'

There was a noise next door and his head shot up. 'Dr Sullivan, need any help in there?'

The blonde head came around the curtain. 'Not at all. Line in, benzodiazepine in, airway maintained and just waiting for a slot at CT.' She glanced down at Liam's patient. 'I would go old-school and think meningitis right now. If you have no history, best to start there.'

His mouth opened, because that was entirely where he was going to start, but he didn't get a chance to respond because her head disappeared behind the curtain again.

'Let's check for a rash and then prep for a lumbar puncture,' he said.

His nurse was smiling at him and he knew that she had picked up on the tension between him and Maggie. He also knew that Maggie had just dealt with a tricky case and put a good suggestion in for his. If they hadn't got off on the wrong foot, he might actually like her.

He got back to business. There was no obvious sign of a rash on their patient as they removed her clothes and put her into a robe. An orderly helped position her on her side, legs pulled up, and the nurse assisted as he inserted the needle into her lower back to collect the cerebrospinal fluid. It should be clear. It wasn't.

Liam and his nurse gave a sigh and handed the sample over to another staff member. 'Urgent lab screen, please.' The staff member disappeared.

Liam looked over the young girl. 'Weight estimate about 115 pounds?'

His nurse nodded. He made some quick calculations and tapped his medicine orders into the tablet. 'We're going to start IV antibiotics. Can you make them up, please? I don't want to wait. Let's get these started straight away.'

He looked up at the clerk. 'Can we try and get hold of the next of kin? I'd be happy to talk to them.'

He bent over the pale face. Barely eighteen. Her life was just beginning and yet this event could mean it was over. Meningitis was scary. Because a lot of people were now vaccinated, the words 'meningitis' didn't create fear the way it had done when he was a boy.

A boy in his class had died in Ireland. Another kid from a family he knew in Dublin had lost fingers and toes. From the look of the cerebrospinal fluid, meningitis seemed the most likely suspect, but that didn't mean he liked a quick diagnosis, not when it could be potentially devastating.

The next few hours were crucial, and although he could have transferred her care to someone else he wanted to see things through as much as possible. He spoke to her parents, who were on their way, her blood pressure and pulse remained steady, her conscious state remained the same. It could take hours for that to improve. Finally, one of the ITU staff came down to take her upstairs. He gave a sigh as she was transferred and headed to the staff lounge.

It was busier than normal and he could see why. A large box of doughnuts was in the middle of the table. One of the team's wives worked in a popular doughnut shop and regularly handed in the 'imperfect' stock.

He'd barely lifted one out of the box when someone thumped down beside him on the chair, lifting a large, misshapen chocolate doughnut out of the box. Maggie.

'Tumour,' she said. One word. But he knew exactly what that meant.

'What age is the kid?'

'Not had her second birthday yet.' She took a big bite of the doughnut and he watched as chocolate cream perilously spilled out of one of the holes.

'Have you handed her over?'

She shot him an are-you-for-real glance, and he inwardly cringed. If she hadn't handed this kid's care over to someone else, she wouldn't be in here.

'Crossan,' she said. 'Is she any good?'

He paused. Maggie was new, and she wouldn't yet know who the good doctors were in each department. It was a terrible thing to say, but most nurses and doctors, if they were getting wheeled into hospital on a gurney, would have a list of people they would want to treat them, and a list of those they wouldn't want to touch them. This was just life.

'Only been here for a year. But seems good,' he replied.

'She'd better be.' Maggie sighed as she caught

the about-to-drip chocolate cream with one of her fingers.

She sucked the cream from her finger then turned to him. He'd been staring—even though he hadn't meant to—and jerked slightly at being caught.

'What?' she said. 'Don't worry, my hands are clean. I'm a fastidious hand-washer.'

He burst out laughing. He couldn't help it.

'What?' she said again, her eyes fixing on his.

He shook his head. 'That word. I can't believe you actually used it.'

'What's wrong with fastidious?'

'It's like a word you would have used in your English exam at school. Not one you use in every-day life.'

She gave him a haughty look, but he could tell it was entirely deliberate to annoy him. 'Maybe some of us just have a better vocabulary than others.'

He leaned forward, resting his elbows on his legs. 'Maybe you do. But I might challenge you about that.'

'Aw, honey,' said one of the EMTs, standing up and taking another doughnut. 'You just fell into Liam's trap.' He walked away, shaking his head and laughing.

Maggie frowned. Some of the others had looked up and were grinning at her. Now she looked indignant. 'I can assure you I'm not falling for—' she glanced at him as if he'd tried to steal the doughnut from her hand '—Liam's trap.'

'Too late,' grinned Abby, one of the senior charge nurses. 'Now we'll take bets on who wins the challenge.'

'What even is the challenge?' Maggie's hands were thrown out in clear exasperation.

Liam grinned at the rest of the staff. 'I guess the challenge for Maggie and me will be to use an "unusual" word in everyday conversation with each other. Has to happen every day and if someone forgets, then they lose the challenge.'

Maggie's voice lowered. 'What's the winner get?'

Liam cleared his throat and pointed to the box of doughnuts. 'The winner gets to keep their pride. The loser,' he pulled a face, 'has to supply the staff room with goodies.'

Abby touched Maggie's shoulder. 'No pressure, Maggie, but I won my round.'

'What was your round?'

Abby smiled. 'Movie quotes. You know, like "*Hasta la vista, baby,*" or "*We're gonna need a bigger boat.*" There were ten seconds to identify the quote and,' she blew on her hand and wiped it on her chest, 'I believe I was the winner, wasn't I, Liam?'

He made a noise that resembled a harrumph.

One of the other nurses rolled her eyes. 'Well, I lost my round. But I will always dispute the final outcome.' She headed to the door and gave Liam a theatrical dirty look.

'You're a sore loser, Kim,' he joked as she left.

Maggie sat back again and this time he got a whiff of her perfume. It was rich, with notes of amber. No light floral scents here. Everything about Maggie screamed a woman who meant business. Which was probably why they would continue to clash.

She took another bite of her doughnut. 'You honestly think you can win this thing?'

He nodded. 'Absolutely.' Liam knew that at times his confidence drove others nuts. But he half wanted it to.

He didn't normally clash with other doctors. He didn't often see them as rivals. His original thoughts about Maggie had been that she was a doctor who had made a mistake, and now he realised that was wrong he should probably apologise.

But apologies were the one thing that Liam knew he wasn't that good at.

He'd get to it, at some point.

Maggie pulled a list from her pocket. 'I have a few things I wanted to go over with you.'

He shifted in his seat and glanced around the staff room, where there were still a few people sitting. 'Should we do this in my office?'

'Probably.' She said it with the air of a person who didn't really care where she was having this conversation—she just knew she was going to have it.

He stood swiftly. 'Let's go, then.'

The walk to his office was short, and Maggie sat the list down on the desk in front of her. She didn't wait to be invited to talk. 'Look, I know I'm new here but there are a few things I need to bring up.'

He steadied himself in his chair, wondering what to make of his new colleague. She had spark, appeared to be quick-thinking, but she certainly didn't fear challenges. He couldn't remember anyone else who'd come at him with a list on their second day in the job.

Maggie kept talking. 'I get that this is an old building, and I also appreciate that the majority of the equipment is brand-new. But old buildings have problems.'

'Such as?'

'Your internet is terrible. I prescribed something for a patient today and it didn't instantly transfer into the tablet my colleague was holding. We can't afford patient delays.' She stared at the nearby walls. 'I understand that these are probably solid stone and brick walls, which isn't helping things, but you're going to have to get your IT guys to find you a more workable solution.'

Of all the things he might have expected, this would never have been on the list.

She held up her hands. 'I ordered the CT scan

for my toddler down in the ER. By the time we got up there in the lift, it was only just sending through the system.'

He gave a nod. 'You're right, there have been issues with the technology. I asked the infrastructure team to come back to me. I'm still waiting.'

She gave him a hard stare. 'I'm no expert, but even I know the basics. You must be able to get something to boost the signal down here.'

He blinked. 'I can ask.'

'Or,' she continued, 'forget the internet and get sim cards put in all your devices. You can pay for sim cards that connect to the best available network, rather than just one, and it opens your chances of getting a better signal.'

He shifted in his chair. 'Do you have an interest in technology?'

She shrugged. 'Usually only for the equipment I use at work. But that's the thing with these hospitals in the US. Most of the buildings have been up for a long time. There were similar issues in the last place I worked in New York. Surely it's better to try and find a solution?'

Was she letting him know that as head of department he should have been all over this?

'Oh, and the mortuary.' She gave a wave of her hand and he swallowed, trying not to pull a face. Was this when he should apologise?

'It's virtually impossible to find. There are no signs. Has no one in this place thought about hanging a sign anywhere? Or maybe everyone has worked here for years, and knows where everything is. But yesterday? Was a disaster.'

He expected her to talk about the patient, but she missed that part entirely.

'And those energy-saving lights that don't come on until you're actually under them are also a disaster. It's like walking through the set of a horror movie. There's no way I would want to escort a family down there at night. It's unprofessional.'

The hairs on the back of his neck stood on end. Unprofessional. The word every single doctor or nurse absolutely hates to hear.

She wasn't describing him. But she was describing his hospital, which more or less could be the same thing.

'Hospitals are the biggest energy users in most cities. Any way that greener methods can be used is surely a bonus in this day and age.'

'But your greener lights don't seem safe. Surely some low-level lighting at all times is more energy efficient than those that don't come on until you're under them?'

He took a breath and didn't reply straight away. Liam wasn't entirely sure what the correct answer was here. He had colleagues he could ask, but he didn't know the answer right now, and was loath to say anything that could prove to be wrong at a later time.

He licked his lips. ‘Anything else?’

Those green eyes of hers had a hint of amusement about them. Was she doing this to annoy him? Or maybe this was her way of getting her own back for yesterday. And he might actually deserve it.

But the jury was still out on Maggie Sullivan. The person he’d spoken to on the phone yesterday had definitely been hiding something.

She was dressed in her scrubs. Scrubs that were so thin that they didn’t hide much. But Maggie had some muscle definition around her arms and possibly her thighs that made him think she either went to the gym, or was a runner.

There was no ring on her finger. And she hadn’t mentioned another half. He decided to start his own line of questioning.

‘You took the job at short notice. Did you have a reason to come to Chicago? Do you have family here?’

She blinked and for the first time didn’t look so keen to talk. Her blonde hair was shiny with hints of pale red, and one strand kept escaping from her ponytail band.

‘No, no family.’

‘And you managed to find a place to stay with no trouble?’

Her stare was so direct it was clear she was wondering why he was going down this line of questioning. 'I found a place. Not entirely sure how good it is.'

'Whereabouts?'

Her gaze narrowed slightly and he raised his hand. 'You've come here at short notice, and you've just told me you don't have family here. I'm assuming you don't know Chicago well?'

She shook her head.

'Then the only reason I'm asking is because some areas are better than others. I can probably give you the background info you need.'

She looked slightly more comfortable now and named the area where she was staying. 'Actually, I was wondering if there's some place around there I can go running? A track? A park?'

He was doing his best not to let his face tell a thousand stories. 'That area can be…challenging.' Seemed like the best word without trying to scare her.

She raised her eyebrows at him.

'Just promise me you won't go running after dark.'

'Wow.' She leaned back in her chair and looked a little defeated. 'And here I was thinking the main problem was the smell.'

'The smell?'

She waved her hand. 'I'll deal with it. Landlord isn't good at answering emails.'

He gave a nod of his head and wondered how much more to ask. 'Do you have friends here?'

She shook her head. 'Don't know anyone here at all.'

Red flags were waving in his head. Why would anyone upend themselves at short notice and come to a city they didn't know, and didn't have any stake in?

What would have to happen in his life to make him do that?

He should actually laugh at himself right now. How was it, when he was being critical of other people, he never applied those rules to himself? A dead brother and the need to run away from every place, and every person that reminded him of that, would be a reason to move to a whole new country, and a whole new city. But he wasn't the one up for debate right now.

'I can give you a note of good running tracks and areas. And for staff that are new to the area, the hospital has a number of groups.'

'You make it sound like I'm the new kid in school with no friends.'

He met her gaze. 'Well…theoretically, you are.' Then—he couldn't help himself—he gave her a wink. 'Like the way I threw that in there?'

'Theoretically? You've got to be joking. That's your effort for today?'

He gave a smile. 'It's a start. But I wasn't joking. There's a book group that takes itself quite seriously. But be warned, it's Tony Adams's turn to pick a book and he always picks a thriller that's at the top of the charts.'

She looked thoughtful. 'I don't mind a thriller.'

'There's also a walking group that might be helpful for exploring some areas, there's another group that volunteers, either at a soup kitchen, one of the animal shelters, or at one of the community groups—that can be youth, or older people.' He waved a finger in the air in a circle. 'They do a kind of rotation thing. Might help you meet some people.'

She stood up and picked up her list. 'I haven't finished with this, but we can do it some other time. I'll think about some of those groups.' She headed to the door and then turned and shot him a smile as her hand was on the door. 'That's if they aren't too preposterous.'

The door clicked behind her and he was left with a smile on his face.

But it fell quickly. His new staff member had just told him she was staying in one of the worst surrounding areas. And she'd clearly left New York in a hurry.

He could hear a low-level alarm sounding at the back of his head. Maggie Sullivan seemed capable and competent, but should he actually be worrying about her?

CHAPTER THREE

IT HAD BEEN nearly two weeks and the smell was steadily getting worse, and the landlord was still ignoring her.

Maggie had started laundering her clothes at a place near the hospital and was sneakily storing some of them in her locker so the smell wouldn't stick. The hospital smelled a whole lot better than her apartment.

She'd decided to leave the rest of her stuff in the shipping depot right now, rather than have it all delivered to the apartment. She loved her sofa. It was like a giant patchwork quilt made of some of the most gorgeous material in the world. Last thing she wanted was for it to smell like this place.

And it seemed as if Liam hadn't been overstepping when he'd warned her about the area. Night-time was not fun. She'd learned not to step outside once it grew dark. It wasn't exactly a great start.

Apart from her initial run-in with Liam, the

rest of the staff at the ER were great. He was definitely a problem though. She'd noticed him double-checking charts yesterday after patients had been discharged—clearly checking other people's work. Didn't he trust the people he worked with? That was odd. Or maybe he was one of those horrid micromanagers. If that was the case, they definitely wouldn't get on.

So far, she'd learned which surgeons thought they ruled the world, and which doctors would bend over backwards to help. She'd learned which rigs the best EMTs were on, and which nurses could do the job with their eyes closed, and which nurses to keep an eye on. There was good and mediocre in every hospital all over the world.

The patients at Chicago weren't too different from other places. Drug, alcohol and homeless issues affected all big cities. General ill-health affected every population, as did road traffic accidents and broken bones.

She was settling into the way of things, and had even contemplated joining the book group that Liam had mentioned. The other thing she had discovered was some of the running trails and tracks.

She was working her way along one now, the 606, which was built on a former railway line. It went through several neighbourhoods but was just under three miles long, which made it a short burst for her.

She was almost at the end, and contemplating where to grab a coffee before work, when she recognised the figure ahead of her.

As he turned his head to the side, she knew instantly it was Liam, but the thing that threw her was the dog. Did Liam Kelly seem like a dog person?

He'd stopped, as his dog had started to sniff something. 'Come on, Barclay,' he muttered. 'We'll be here all day.'

She jogged up alongside him. 'Didn't take you for a dog person.'

He didn't even miss a beat. 'I was completely a dog person until I rescued Barclay. He's made me question my sanity.'

She laughed and bent down to the clearly scent-driven beagle, scratching his neck.

'Watch out,' said Liam. 'He can be a biter.'

'Can he?' Maggie dropped to her knees in front of the tri-colour beagle and stared into his big brown eyes. 'Barclay, are you really a biter?' She ruffled his soft ears and kept talking to him in a low voice. Barclay looked back at her, sniffing her hands, then nuzzled closer.

She looked up at Liam, unbelieving. 'A biter? This dog?'

Liam held up a hand. 'Honestly, he is. He's just playing with you a little. Please be careful. Because I was jogging, I don't have a muzzle on him. If we're walking, he always wears one.'

Maggie stood up and started strolling alongside them, putting her hands on her hips and looking around. 'You live near here?'

'Not quite around here, but Barclay's daycare is close by—on the way to the hospital.'

'Know any good coffee shops? I want to grab something before I start.' She raised her eyebrows at him. 'I work in this place where you might not always get a break.'

He sighed and nodded ahead of them both. 'Bonnacio's is the best coffee place.'

'Do they let dogs in?'

He actually looked a little nervous. 'Like I said, I don't have his muzzle with me.'

She held out her hand for his lead. 'Let me take charge of him. Just call me the dog whisperer.'

For a second she thought he was going to object but then he rolled his eyes, handed the lead over, and opened the door for them.

The Italian coffee shop was cute with checked tablecloths, a glass cabinet full of delicious sandwiches and cakes, and a strong smell of coffee.

He gestured to a table as he walked to the counter. 'What do you want?'

She slung off her backpack and pulled some notes from her wallet. 'Two Americanos. A mozzarella and tomato panini for later, and a chocolate cream aragostine.'

He laughed out loud and waved her money

away. 'Think of this as the dog-sitting fee,' he said and brought over a tray a few minutes later.

Barclay was sitting on the floor next to her, but watching Liam with expectation in his eyes. Sure enough, Liam had brought some cold meat for him and a bowl of water.

'Let me,' said Maggie, taking a sip of her coffee and dangling a strip of meat in the air for Barclay to catch in his teeth.

Liam settled across from her. 'You gave that order like a true Italian coffee-house connoisseur,' he said.

She held out one arm. 'They generally are the best in any city you go to. I hadn't found one yet, so thanks for this.'

She could sense it as his eyes went up and down her apparel. 'You've been running into work?'

She nodded. 'Best way to fit in my exercise.'

He glanced down at her rucksack. 'But you don't run on the way back.' There was a low question in his tone that made her almost smile.

'You're asking me if I go running in my neighbourhood at night?'

He pulled a face as he sipped his latte. 'In a roundabout way,' he admitted.

She pulled a face in return. 'Well,' she said slowly, 'it turns out you might be right about the neighbourhood.'

His gaze remained steady. 'I'm sorry. I know you moved at short notice and didn't have much of a chance to scope the city. But if you decide to look for somewhere else, I, or any of the other folk in the ER, will be happy to give you advice.'

'I signed a lease for six months. I think I will be tied into it, so I guess I'll just have to grin and bear it.'

'I get it,' he said, bending down to scratch Barclay's ears. Barclay gave a little growl.

Maggie started to laugh. 'Did he just growl at you?'

Liam looked down at his dog, who was currently scowling at him. 'Yep, that's pretty normal for him.'

'How does he do at daycare?'

'Oh, he's fine with other dogs. It's just humans he generally doesn't like.'

Maggie felt something wash over her and she bent down again and rubbed his tummy. 'You said he was a rescue?'

Liam nodded.

'You've got to wonder what happened in his life before.'

He gave a little shudder. He was wearing a dark green running shirt made of that shiny, sweat-controlling fabric. Trouble with that was that it showed every sinewy bit of muscle on his chest, arms and shoulders as he moved. She had shirts like that and was suddenly glad she wasn't wearing one.

As she looked back down at Barclay, she glanced under the table. Now he'd sat down, his grey running shorts had lifted a bit to reveal muscular thighs and toned legs. She sighed. She didn't really like this guy. Why was she stealing glances at his body?

Maggie straightened in her chair and focused on the chocolate cream aragostine. It was truly worthy of her attention.

'The shelter didn't know much about his background. They suspected he might have come from a lab—a lot of beagles do. But he'd also been returned a few times because of his biting.'

'So, you willingly took a biter?' Now she was surprised. Was there actually a heart inside that bristly exterior?

His brow wrinkled slightly. 'Yes, he was the one that wouldn't get adopted. Of course I took him.'

She leaned back in her chair, folded her arms and watched him carefully. 'I wouldn't have taken you for a dog smooch.'

'A what?' He leaned towards her with confusion on his face.

She sipped her first Americano again. 'A dog smooch. You don't seem like one.'

'What on earth is a dog smooch? I've never heard that before.' Then his gaze narrowed.

'Wait…we only play that game at work. And I've never heard that word before. Did you just make it up?'

She gave a half-snort. 'You think I'd make a word up to beat you at a game I'm primed to win? And no, I know you only play that at work. You like an audience.'

Any trace of amusement that had been on his face dropped off. 'I what?'

'You like an audience. If you're telling someone off, or if you want to get a point across—you like an audience.'

She could tell she'd annoyed him, and she wondered if she'd been too upfront. But this guy had annoyed her from the start. Plus, she'd started to notice his body. It was best if she tried to keep everything at arm's length between them.

'I do not,' he spat back. It was almost a hiss. Whether she'd meant it or not, she'd hit a nerve.

'I took you into my office to speak to you.'

'But not before you'd dressed me down in front of two cops and a dead guy.' There was the tiniest twitch at the side of his mouth, and she wondered if he might have wanted to smile there.

She kept going. 'And I noticed you doing it with one of the surgical interns the other day, and that guy from Radiology.'

He blinked and took a second to clearly gather himself. 'The guy from Radiology was about to make a schoolboy error, and the surgical intern made a mark on the wrong side of someone's body. You think I shouldn't call these people out?'

She watched him for a few moments, drumming her fingers on the table before taking the final mouthful of the first Americano. 'I think it's more about the *way* you do it.' Then she added, 'Even when you're wrong.'

'Okay.' He sighed and lifted one hand. 'I thought you'd declared someone dead who wasn't. I realise that wasn't you.'

'Only because I told you.'

'I would have realised eventually.'

She started on her second Americano, letting the hot coffee boost her senses. 'Not good enough.'

He shook his head for a moment as if his brain was telling him a hundred things and looked at her in exasperation. 'You are so…succinct.'

She shot him a suspicious glance. 'Are you playing the game?'

'No.'

'Just checking!' She smiled, crossing her legs and holding up both hands. She still had the lead around her wrist, but Barclay was lying under the table now. She didn't believe this dog was ever naughty.

She studied him for a second and decided to finish the pastry. It was just too good to leave, and it was likely he would fall out with her soon.

She squeezed out a little of the chocolate cream onto one finger and held it under the table for Barclay to lick.

'Chocolate and cream,' he said in a stern voice. 'Two things dogs shouldn't get.'

'You're the kind of guy who doesn't buy pup cups, aren't you?'

She folded her panini in the napkin on the table and slid it into her rucksack. That was her lunch for later and she didn't plan on leaving it behind.

'Succinct is an interesting word. I guess I will agree that I'm direct. I call things as I see them.'

'And that's all I was doing with the surgical intern and the radiography student. These are people lives we're dealing with. We can't make mistakes.'

'Agreed,' she said. 'But you can do it in a supportive way. You don't have that gift. Or, if you do, I haven't seen it yet.'

He leaned back in his chair. Did he actually just scowl at her? 'Is it wrong to expect people who are trained and earning a living to really just do the job they're supposed to do, and do it safely?' He folded his arms. 'For me, that's an absolute minimum.'

She decided to just go for the throat burn and finish the second Americano all at once.

'We just clearly have different methods.' She managed to get the words out, even though her throat was spasming. She gave him a smile, along with a half-laugh. 'I'm just surprised they don't all hate you.'

She crouched down to give Barclay the rest of the cold meat and another scratch behind the ears. 'You really are a very good dog,' she said in a low voice to him. 'I'd like to meet you again.'

Barclay gave a little noise. It was a cross between a sigh and a whimper.

She saw Liam's calf muscle clench. 'I really don't know why he's like this with you,' he muttered.

'He can sense the love from me.' She grinned, even though she knew it would just drive him crazy. That was actually part of the fun. Seeing how much she could wind Liam Kelly up could be her new pastime. 'It emanates from my very pores,' she said as she stood and then pointed her finger. 'And no, I'm still not playing the game.'

'Emanate wouldn't count.'

'I think I could make it.' She handed over the lead. 'If my lease let me have pets I'd steal him from you.' Then she shook her head. 'But no. I wouldn't subject him to my place. If he gets flung out of daycare let me know and I'll see if I can help you with him. I could walk him some time if we're on opposite shifts.'

He gave her a somewhat incredulous stare. 'You spend the whole time picking a fight with me, then openly try to steal my dog?'

Maggie grinned. 'What can I say? I like to put

my cards on the table. Bye, Barclay.' She gave the dog a wave as she headed out of the door.

Liam Kelly watched as his colleague in her raspberry pink T-shirt and black leggings disappeared out of the coffee shop, tugged her backpack onto her shoulders and started jogging again. Had that really all just happened?

He was trying to make sense of everything in his head as Barclay sat and looked at him as if he was entirely stupid.

The dog could be right.

He finished his coffee and headed to the doggy daycare to drop Barclay off before his shift. It was clear that Maggie was going to get there before him and he wondered if this was going to be a day of fireworks.

But here was the thing. He wasn't dreading it. He was actually looking forward to it.

There were twenty patients waiting in the ER by the time he arrived. Some had been triaged but were still to be assessed, some were waiting for tests, and the rest waiting for test results.

'This place is backed up when it really shouldn't be,' said Maggie as she walked past him. Her hair was coiled up in some clasps and instead of the regular pale green scrubs, she was wearing some pink ones today.

'Going somewhere special?' he asked.

She looked down. 'Just fancied a change of

colour. And since I'm buying them myself, I figured I could buy any colour I like.'

'You're buying your own scrubs?'

She looked at him and rubbed the V part at her neck. 'Don't you find the hospital ones scratchy?'

His hand went automatically to his front shoulder—and he started scratching. 'I don't know what you mean,' he deadpanned.

She turned her back to him. 'Touch them.'

His eyes widened and he pulled back a little.

'I mean it,' she said, tapping her shoulder. 'Touch them.'

So he did, reaching one hand out and touching the smooth-as-silk fabric. As soon as she saw the recognition on his face she grinned. 'See? These beauties were designed to be worn all day, without leaving any sore bits.'

He wrinkled his nose. 'I don't want to think where the sore bits are.'

'And you don't have to.' She ran her hand down the front of her scrub top. 'Because I have these.' And even though she was clearly happy, she frowned in annoyance.

He knew instantly what was going on and grinned. 'Can't think of an unusual enough word for them?'

'No,' she admitted.

'Even better.' He looked around. 'Let's try and get some people moving. Can you review everyone in curtains one to ten, and I'll review eleven to twenty.'

She picked up the nearest chart. 'Sounds like a challenge. You're on.'

For the next hour he heard her thick accent giving instructions and saw the occasional flash of pink on the way past. He was busy enough with his own patients, and stopped to help with two ambulance arrivals that required the patients to go to Resus.

When he passed one of the cubicles, he could see her with a young school-age kid and a worried parent. Whether she realised it or not, the staff were reporting how astute she was with kids. There had been nothing specific in her résumé about paediatrics, but even he could see how good she was with them.

Something about this little girl caught his eye. She was pale with a slightly withered look about her. He could hear Maggie asking questions and see her noting the responses. The little girl had a white blob of cream near one of her elbows, indicating the numbing cream had been put there to allow them to take bloods.

'She's not been herself, she's so tired all the time, and she has no energy.'

'Is she eating and drinking?'

'Anything and everything.' The mother sighed.

'Has she lost weight?'

The mum frowned. 'Well… I think she might have. But I'm not sure.'

'Any other unusual symptoms?'

The mum gave a furtive glance at her daughter. 'She wet the bed the other night. She hasn't done that since she was a toddler. Could it be a urinary-tract infection?'

Liam knew exactly what Maggie would be thinking and he moved quickly, first to bring a jug of water and a glass, and secondly to pull a machine from a nearby drawer.

He smiled as he shifted the curtains with his shoulder and set the water and glass down, pouring some for the little girl. He handed the machine to Maggie.

She didn't say a word, just took the machine and unzipped a little pouch.

'The tiredness and all the sleeping…is it one of those blood cancers? Could it be leukaemia?'

Rachel, her daughter, leaned forward and drained the glass of water. 'I'm going to do a little finger-prick test on you, Rachel,' Maggie said calmly. 'And then I'm sure we'll know exactly what's going on.'

'Will it hurt?' came the shaky voice.

'Maybe just for a second,' said Maggie, then she stuck a small strip into the machine, took another device and held it next to Rachel's finger. Rachel flinched, then Maggie gently squeezed a spot of blood from her finger onto the strip. There were a few short beeps, then a longer one. Maggie turned the screen to Liam.

She turned to Rachel's mum. 'It looks like Rachel has diabetes. Is there any history of it in the family?'

The woman paused for a moment, started to shake her head and then stopped. 'My aunt,' she said.

Maggie nodded. 'Okay, Rachel's sugar levels are really high right now, so we are going to give her some medicine and bring them down. We'll also need to take some blood tests and admit her up to Paediatrics.'

'She's going to have to have injections?' The mum looked scared.

'There are lots of new ways to look after diabetes these days,' said Maggie. 'One of our nurses is diabetic. She wears a monitor that keeps an eye on her blood sugar and a small pump attached to her body gives insulin as required. I'll get her to come and talk to you. The staff in Paediatrics will explain everything.'

She frowned as Liam started speaking to Rachel around the other side of the bed. He peeled back the clear dressing covering the cream and wiped it off. Within a few seconds he had slid a small cannula into place and withdrawn three bottles of blood, before taping the cannula safely in place.

'Told you it wouldn't be sore,' he said in a low

voice to Rachel, who was nodding in wonder. ‘That cream is magic.’

He held up the bottles to her mother. ‘We need to get these to the lab to see how Rachel’s kidneys are doing.’ He gave a nod to Maggie. ‘I’ll leave you to sort out the initial dose of insulin before we hand over to Paeds. I don’t want any delays.’

Maggie’s face was entirely expressionless but he could sense the fury leaking from her pores right now. He wasn’t doing anything wrong. It was essential these children were treated straight away or they ran the risk of falling into a coma. Maggie would know that, and maybe he was overstepping. But he’d happily take a shouting match later than let anything happen in his ER.

Maggie gave him a smile that didn’t reach those green eyes. ‘Don’t worry, Dr Kelly, I have everything under control.’

Yep. He was in trouble.

He ran the bloods to the lab himself and phoned up to paeds to ask their attending to come down.

‘I was just paged. I’ll be down in an hour.’

‘You’ll be down now and get a potentially keto-acidotic child on a regime to ensure her condition doesn’t worsen.’

There was a pause at the end of the line. Liam knew he sometimes intimidated the attendings. He also knew that when some attendings specialised they thought they were lord of their own manors, and didn't like to take instruction from anyone else.

'Okay,' came the response, followed by a click of the phone.

He took a breath. Okay indeed. It was time to step back and let others do their job.

He moved down the corridor and picked up one of his charts. He still needed to free up some cubicle space.

He started seeing a few more patients, then checked some of the resident's charts, seeing something he wasn't sure about.

'Ken,' he called, 'can you come here?'

A worried-looking resident appeared at his side. 'Is something wrong?'

'This patient. Are they still here?'

'I turned them over to Surgical.'

He answered as though it was a question.

'Without waiting for all the test results?'

Maggie appeared as if by magic at his side. She glanced over the chart and smiled at Ken. 'Good call, Ken. Looks like a classic appendix. Don't want to wait about with those guys.'

Liam frowned. 'But,' he glared at Maggie, 'we like to wait until we have the full picture. The lab results and scan would have given confirmation.'

'And the lab results will still be processed, and the scan will still happen,' she butted in, smiling again at Ken and giving him a nod. 'And in the meantime, the surgical team will hopefully have more expertise than the rest of us in controlling the pain from a possible appendicitis, and judging when it might rupture.'

She shot Liam a look he'd now definitely seen more than once. 'Well done, Ken,' she said, tapping him on the shoulder. 'Keep up the good work.'

Ken, who finally looked relieved, relaxed his shoulders and practically sprinted down the corridor to get away.

Liam pressed his lips together. 'Want to tell me why you did that?'

She looked him clear in the eye. 'Because you were checking charts and about to give him trouble for not waiting for results. For showing initiative—which we want residents to do.'

'For making a judgement call that could be wrong, and he potentially doesn't have enough experience for,' said Liam.

'Stop,' she said quietly, and pointed to the empty hall. 'Did you see his face? How scared he was? How he couldn't wait to get away from you?'

She rested her hand on his arm. Warm, skin-to-skin contact. 'I want these residents…' She gave her head a shake. 'I want *our* residents to have the confidence to act, and to have the confidence to come and ask for help if they think they need it.'

'And I want everything done correctly, no mistakes. I'll make the call if they are ready to make those kinds of decisions. Don't you know that now they tend to observe the patient for twenty-four hours with IV antibiotics, rather than rush everyone to surgery, because it leads to better outcomes?'

She nodded. 'Yep, and can't say I agree with it. Leaving a patient in pain, when there is also a chance of rupture, doesn't really work for me.' She winked at him. 'Just as well I'm not a surgeon, then, isn't it?'

He opened his mouth to argue but realised there wouldn't be much point. He was still trying to process the fact she'd used the terms *ours* when referring to the residents.

Her grip on his arm tightened a little. 'And just so we're clear, I have no problem with routine audits. But if I see you hanging over my shoulder, second-guessing me when I have a patient, I will send you on your way, and I won't worry about who overhears. Your time is better spent with your own patients.'

Liam could easily have a stand-up fight right now, but as he looked at the board he realised with a sigh that he likely could get through a number of these patients.

He picked up the first chart. The man had been triaged and had been waiting more than four hours to be seen. His symptoms were vague. Nothing jumped out at him, and Liam did kind of wonder why this guy was here.

He pulled back the curtain and stood at the side of the bed. 'Mr Bennett?'

The man, in his late twenties, nodded. He was wearing a suit, but the tie had been loosened and the top buttons of his shirt opened.

'Can you tell me what brought you here today?'

He looked up at Liam. 'I don't know. I just don't feel right.'

Liam held in his breath. He hated to stereotype. But there were certain kinds of patients. They had the daytripper, who appeared with vague symptoms that never amounted to much, generally had a few tests, then went home.

Then therc were the hypochondriacs, who had generally watched an episode of whatever was the favourite medical TV show of the moment, and had developed all the symptoms of a disease that only twenty people in the world had ever had, since they'd watched the show the night before.

If a farmer appeared and said he didn't quite feel right—or said that his wife had told him to come—doctors and nurses alike knew to run for the emergency trolley.

Mr Bennett wasn't a farmer, but Liam wondered if he might fall into one of the other two categories.

He started running through a list of things with Mr Bennett as he connected him to a blood-pressure monitor and checked his temperature. His answers were still vague or negative to many of the main symptoms that people might present with.

But, as Liam asked permission to start a physical exam, and began feeling around Mr Bennett's neck and throat—mainly to see if he was showing any sign of infection—he noticed something about one of his pupils.

Liam pulled out his penlight and shone it into both eyes. One pupil was much more pinprick than the other.

He examined further, noticing one eyelid appeared to be drooping a little, but it wasn't obvious.

He did other tests on his speech and Mr Bennett's limbs and movements to rule out the possibility of a stroke.

'Tell me other things you've noticed that seem not quite right,' he prompted, noticing a shadow behind him.

'It's stupid really,' said the man.

Liam had pulled out his stethoscope. 'Lean forward until I listen to your chest. Take a breath for me. Good. And now we'll do the back.' He slid the stethoscope around the back of Mr Bennett's shirt and got him to breathe again. 'In for me, and out. Thanks.'

His brain was putting pieces together. Air entry was good but didn't sound entirely even. He slid a saturation probe onto the man's finger and watched the numbers. Ninety-eight was good, but not perfect.

'Tell us again what you noticed,' said the voice with a Scottish accent beside him. He could see Mr Bennett concentrate for a second to catch all the words. 'Nothing you tell us is stupid.'

Maggie moved around to Mr Bennett's other side as she glanced at his chart and the notes Liam had made so far. He could feel himself bristle, but reminded himself that he'd done the same to her earlier.

'Everything okay with our other patient?'

'Everything's peachy. She's gone up to the ward.' It was the way she said the word *peachy*. Somehow, he knew that wasn't in her normal vocabulary and the whole episode had likely not been peachy.

Maggie turned her attention back to their patient. She looked at the chart. 'So, Stephen, tell me what's happening with you that you think is silly.'

He sighed and rubbed one side of his face. 'I don't even know if it's real, but I thought that last night, when I did a workout, only one side of my face was sweating.'

Stephen had his eyes downcast, which meant that when Maggie rolled hers at Liam, he knew exactly why.

She leaned in front of Stephen's face and whipped out her own pen torch and shone the light in both eyes, then touched one of his eyelids.

'Have you injured your face at all? Had a ball in the face? Anything like that?'

Stephen shook his head. 'No—why?'

She touched his arm. 'Well, Dr Kelly here is just about to tell you that you might have something called Horner's syndrome. It's a condition that some people can have from birth, or it can develop later, and it means that the nerve pathways to your eyes have been affected and disrupted in some way, meaning one of your pupils is reacting differently, one of your eyelids is drooping a little and it would explain why you only felt sweat on one side of your face.'

Stephen shook his head and touched his eye. 'But why's this happened?'

'There are a number of possible reasons for this, Stephen,' Liam cut in—after all, this was his patient, 'and if it's okay with you, I'd like to run another few tests.'

He picked up the tablet and ordered a chest X-ray, some blood tests and a scan of the carotid arteries. Then he picked up an otoscope to examine Stephen's ears for any sign of infection—there was none.

'I'll get one of the nurses to check on you, and we'll,' he said the word with irritation, 'be back to check up on you soon.'

He gave a nod to Maggie and held the curtain for her to exit.

She gave him a furious stare and strode down

the corridor, waiting until they were clear of people and were standing off to one side.

'Let's be honest. Were you checking up on me earlier? I am perfectly capable of diagnosing a child with diabetes.'

'I'm sure you are. Were you checking up on me?'

She folded her arms. 'No, I was coming to give you a piece of my mind.'

'Again?'

The green eyes sparked with fury. 'I might have mentioned this before, but the way you speak to people doesn't just affect you.'

'What are you talking about?'

'I just had to deal with that two-bit hustler from Paediatrics. You'd annoyed him, and then he came down with an attitude and could have upset my patient and her mother.'

'Did he?'

'No, because I pulled him out from the curtain and told him exactly what I thought of him and his attitude. And how, right then, when a little girl and her mother were clearly terrified about this potential diagnosis, how he acted right now would stay with them for the rest of their lives.'

Liam stopped for a moment and almost smiled. It was a good point and it sounded as if she'd made it well. He was amused. 'Did you just call him a two-bit hustler?'

Maggie sighed. 'I worked with a nurse from Texas once. She called everyone that annoyed her a two-bit hustler and I've kind of stuck with it.' She shrugged. 'I might even have called him that to his face, so there could be a complaint.'

He could tell from her demeanour that she didn't give a damn if the guy complained about her.

'What? If I use a Scottish saying they rarely know what I mean. Crabbit bampot, eejit, skiver, and blootered numpty just don't have the same effect in New York,' she looked around, 'or, I suspect, in Chicago.'

'Two-bit hustler it is, then.' He nodded in agreement.

The eyebrows lifted briefly in a moment of challenge. 'I'm flabbergasted you're letting me get away with that one.'

It was Liam's turn to raise his eyebrows. 'Flabbergasted?'

He could tell she was trying so hard not to smile. 'Quite,' she replied.

'You're being quite quizzical today.'

She wagged her finger. 'Oh, no, I don't think that one works,' but her gaze narrowed and she gave a him a stern look.

'I don't think we established why you were checking up on me, or,' she kept her finger wagging, 'why you nearly missed an obvious diagnosis. A medical student could have got that one. We all tell jokes about people with half their face sweating.'

Now she was definitely trying to annoy him.

'You just came in and stole the glory of the diagnosis. And let's not forget what this might mean for this guy. His breath sounds were uneven. He could have a chest tumour.'

'What age is he?' It was as if she had instantly forgotten they were sparring and was more concerned about the patient. Which was exactly what he wanted from all his doctors.

'Twenty-nine.'

'Should we get him to phone a relative? So there is someone here for support in case he gets bad news?'

'I think that would be a good idea. But I should have that conversation with him. I am his doctor.'

Maggie thought for a moment. He actually felt as if he could see her brain ticking. Her face went through a multitude of tiny expressions. This lady should never play poker—but she probably knew that.

'Yes, you should.' She put her hand on his arm. 'Good luck, Liam. That could be a tough conversation.'

And with that she turned and walked away.

Liam was momentarily stunned. She fought with him on every occasion about anything.

But here, she had just backed down.

And he got it, and he was actually grateful, because he knew as soon as he told Stephen he should contact someone to come in, that the young man would realise something else could be on the cards.

Maggie Sullivan continued to surprise him every day.

CHAPTER FOUR

SHE'D LOOKED AT four other apartments now. Of course, she couldn't get out of the lease she was currently in, but she was trying to pretend there would be a loophole somewhere. The worst part was, she felt as if she was starting to smell like the place.

On a positive note, she spent as little time here as humanly possible. She'd joined the book group, which held meetings in a variety of coffee shops throughout the city. So far she'd read a thriller, a romance and a science-fiction novel. She'd also found a shelter to volunteer at, to fill the animal-shaped hole in her life. She only did three or four hours every week, and she did want to bring all the cats and dogs home with her, but the snuggles were worth it.

Things at work were still…feisty. And she couldn't put her finger on exactly why.

Maggie had never been one to tolerate fools gladly. Most of the staff she worked with were fine. She loved working with students, and didn't mind teaching or explaining things to someone who didn't understand. She hated arrogance and entitlement, but neither of those words described Liam. But every time she came into contact with him, he just seemed to put her hackles up. It could be the mildest sentence, about the most irrelevant thing, and it just seemed to send fireworks up for her.

And it was only ever him. She wasn't sure what it was about Liam Kelly that just made the sparks fly the way they did.

She was still pretending she hadn't noticed how good-looking he was. She was still pretending that his Irish accent didn't send messages to parts of her body that she was ignoring. Because if she started going down that road…she didn't know where it could end.

Men were off-limits for Maggie Sullivan. She couldn't trust her own judgement any more. Her brain at night spun with all the signs that she'd missed with her ex. All the so-easy things that he'd said that were clearly lies. The excuses. The missed dates. The ignored texts and phone calls.

Maggie had never really been a suspicious type of person. She wasn't the sort of woman who met a man and rearranged her whole life around them. She had her own friends, her own interests, so if he missed a call or a text she didn't immediately decide something else was going on. Clearly, she should have.

So she didn't trust her own judgement any more. She'd got things so wrong once, who was to say she wouldn't do it again?

She hadn't heard anyone mention that Liam had a wife or a partner. He didn't wear a ring, but that didn't mean anything. And he did have a dog—and he took it to daycare. Surely if he'd had a partner they would help with Barclay?

What was she doing? Why was she even thinking about him? She didn't like him. She didn't like him at all. Or maybe just a little.

The phone rang just as she was about to go for a run. And when she heard the Irish accent, she immediately assumed something was wrong at work.

'Liam? What's wrong? Do you need me to cover a shift?'

'Yes, and no.'

'What does that mean?'

'I mean that doggy daycare won't take Barclay because he was sick outside. And then he had… well, you know.'

'Do you need me to take him to the vet?'

'I don't think so. Maybe? He seems fine. He's just in a huff.'

'He's in a huff because he's with you. He'll be fine with me.' She was smiling now. A little dog-love might be exactly what she needed.

'So you'll look after him?'

'Sure, why don't you just head to the ER and I'll meet you outside?'

'Are you sure?'

'No problem.'

Half an hour later, an embarrassed Liam was standing outside the ER with Barclay, who looked as if he could cartwheel around the place.

'Is he feeling better?'

Liam ran one hand through his hair. 'I have absolutely no idea.' He dug into his pocket. 'Here are the keys to my house.'

She stared at them in her hand as he rhymed off his address. 'Well, I can't expect you to take Barclay back to your place in case he is sick again.'

'Or the other thing,' she murmured.

'Yes, let's not go there.' He handed her a pile of poo bags. 'I'll take him to the park first, walk about and see how he does. What should I give him to eat?'

'Just his regular food. It's at my house. He's never had a problem with it before.'

Maggie gave a nod as she bent down and rubbed Barclay's ears. He seemed delighted to see her.

'Okay, what time do you finish?'

'Ten.' And then his face fell. 'Oh, that's late… it will be dark. I'll walk you home.'

'I'll get a cab.'

'I'll pay for it.'

She opened her mouth, ready to fight with him again, and then decided not to bother. 'We can talk about that later.'

She gave a wee tug of the lead. 'Come on then, pup. Let's see how you're doing.'

Liam took a deep breath and bent down to pat Barclay, dropping a kiss on his head. 'Hope you're okay, fellow,' he said quietly, and Maggie was impressed to hear the obvious affection in his voice. 'Phone me if there's any problem and I'll get him booked in at the vet's.'

Maggie gave a nod, and a wave, and started down the street with Barclay.

She'd only taken a few steps when she ran into one of the nurses, Carol.

Carol looked suspiciously at Barclay. 'Isn't that Liam's dog?'

Maggie nodded. 'Yep, he's sick and daycare refused him, so I offered to look after him. I love dogs,' she said simply.

Carol folded her arms and looked her up and down. 'Oh, no, girl. I thought you were too clever for that.'

'For what?'

Carol waved a hand. 'For falling for short-term-lease Liam.'

Maggie burst out laughing. 'What did you just call him?'

Carol was indignant. 'Short-term-lease Liam. It's what we all call him. He has more girlfriends than most guys have hot dinners. All beautiful. All lovely. And before you get to find out anything about them, he's dumped them.'

'Maybe they've dumped him?' said Maggie. Hoping that a few women had held Liam to account.

Carol shook her head. 'That man has never dated for more than a few months. Not in the whole time I've known him. And I've been here five years.' She wagged her finger at Maggie. 'So don't you go and get your heart broken by him.'

Now it was Maggie's turn to shake her head. 'Let me just shoot that rumour down. I'm the dog-sitter. That's it.' She bent down and rubbed Barclay's nose. 'And if Barclay wants to break my heart, so be it. Because I'm off men right now. Too much trouble.'

Carol gave her a sigh, and a suspicious glance and headed to the ER.

Maggie tried not to laugh out loud again at Liam's nickname. So, he never dated for long. Interesting.

She half wondered what Liam would have done if they hadn't met the other day and he knew that Barclay would be okay with her.

But that wasn't her issue. She had a dog to babysit—and a nickname to contemplate.

They went to the park, which had an outdoor café that supplied water for dogs. Barclay sniffed about for a bit and lay down. Then she took him for a walk around the lake, jingling Liam's keys in her hands.

She had no idea where his house was. She'd have to look up his address. Barclay made a little noise and decided to go to the toilet. Maggie pulled a face, picked up what she could, and decided whether she was nervous or not she was taking him home.

Liam lived in an actual house. In the city, in downtown Chicago. Her smelly apartment could fit eight times over in his home. A traditional brick and masonry mansion with a gorgeous front room, a huge kitchen that looked out over a lawn. She didn't climb the stairs to where she imagined the bedrooms might be, because she didn't have reason.

Oh, yes, she was tempted. But she preferred to imagine the house had hidden cameras everywhere and her actions would be noticed.

She did wonder how many of the women he'd dated had seen the inside of his house. All of them? None of them? She shook her head. This was none of her business. She hadn't exactly revealed her own poor judgement and bad dating history, so why should he? Barclay nuzzled at her knee and she bent to rub his floppy ears.

There were two dog beds. One in the kitchen and one in the main room. So, she opened the back kitchen door out to the garden in case Barclay needed to relieve himself, then decided to check the kitchen cupboards and make herself a coffee. She found three packets of chocolate biscuits, all unopened, and only felt marginally guilty about opening her preferred option.

She put out some food for Barclay and refilled his water bowl, but once she settled on the sofa in front of the TV with her coffee and biscuits, Barclay jumped up next to her and put his head on her lap. He even snored a little. Well, actually, a lot.

The day passed quickly. Maggie wished she'd planned ahead and brought a book, but Liam had a few on a shelf in his kitchen, so she grabbed one of those once she'd tired of the TV.

Liam sent her a text around six p.m. How's my boy?

She smiled as she replied. Quiet. He's slept a lot. Is that normal for him?

He's a beagle.

What does that mean?

Yes, it's normal for him. Has he been sick again?

No, but he hasn't been interested in food. Just had some water.

I'm sending you dinner, since I know there is

nothing in my fridge. Chinese? Indian? Pizza? Japanese? Italian?

I could say no, but I'm not proud. Pasta with meatballs please.

Done.

The food arrived, along with a bottle of wine. Maggie swithered for a few moments before finally searching the cupboards again for a wine glass, and the drawers for a corkscrew. There was a second portion of meatballs and pasta, which she left sealed, as she assumed Liam would eat it later.

After a glass of wine, she started to relax a bit more. Barclay went outside again, and she dutifully followed to make sure he wasn't unwell. If he was she'd need to let Liam know when he came back. But Barclay just seemed to pee, and then sniff the entire back garden.

When he came back in, he headed up the stairs.

There was no stairgate, so Maggie had to presume he was allowed up there. What was a girl to do? She followed him, passing a beautiful bathroom, an office, a bedroom and then a bigger one, which was clearly the main bedroom. Barclay was lying on top of the bed, his head on one of the pillows.

There was yet another dog bed on the floor,

but it looked virtually untouched. Barclay clearly slept next to his master.

She could smell Liam's aftershave as she hovered in the doorway. It felt intrusive to walk into the place where he slept, but she took a breath and knelt beside Barclay for a while, stroking his head. It was after nine. Maybe this was his bedtime?

He seemed comfortable. So she decided to go back downstairs to wash her dishes. As she walked down the large carved staircase a photo on the wall made her stop.

It was clearly quite old. The colours in the photo were a little faded. She moved closer. It was clearly Liam, with his arm slung around the shoulders of another boy. They were both dressed in summer clothes and looked around ten or eleven.

There was something about the other boy. He looked similar to Liam, but different. Frailer. Liam hadn't mentioned family. Was this a friend?

There were no other photos and certainly not of any women.

It was none of her business and she knew that, so she padded down the stairs and had just finished washing and putting away the cutlery she'd used when she heard the front door click.

There was a grunt from upstairs, and then some ferocious barking. Barclay came down the stairs like a ball from a cannon, leaping from the third bottom step straight into Liam's arms.

Liam's face lit up. 'Hey boy,' he said as he caught him and staggered back. 'Are you good? Are you feeling better?'

Barclay was licking his face now but squirming in his arms. She had no idea how he was managing to keep a hold of him.

After a few minutes he set him down on the carpet runner, and Barclay growled at him, then trotted back up the stairs.

'What was that about?' asked Maggie in wonder.

Liam waved his hand. 'He's funny about his bedtime. He doesn't like to be disturbed, but always barks and comes to see when the door opens. But once he's seen who it is he's straight back to bed. Nothing gets between him and his sleep.'

Maggie smiled. 'Clearly. You weren't joking when you said that he was the boss.'

Liam laughed and held out his hands. 'This house, it's Barclay's. I just live here to serve him.'

She gave a sigh and said, 'Well, I'm glad he seems okay. If you give me a number I'll call a cab.'

Liam put up his hand. 'Wait, stay for a bit. I mean, if you want to. I'm sorry about today. I never even gave you a chance to prepare. To bring your computer or anything you might need.' His nose twitched. 'Is that pasta I smell?'

She nodded. 'I don't know where you got it from but it was great. I left your portion on the side.'

He moved towards the kitchen. 'Did you finish the wine?'

'What? No!' she laughed. 'I only had half a glass.'

'Well, come and have another half while I eat dinner,' he said, moving through to the kitchen.

She thought about it for about a second, and then decided to join him. He might not eat a whole portion. There could be leftovers. She knew good pasta when she tasted it.

'I'm surprised Barclay hasn't come down for the meatballs,' she remarked as she slid onto the stool opposite him at the kitchen island.

He was picking the lid off his food and sticking it in the microwave to reheat. 'He might still. But he's weird. It's almost like he has an off-switch at night. He will spend all day sniffing continuously and always looking for food, but come nine o'clock at night—you better not get in the way of his bed.'

She was leaning on the counter and staring at him. It was odd being in his environment. This wasn't a glass house. It was definitely a home. She'd found three dog beds so far. But apart from the photo on the stairs, she hadn't seen anything to do with family. Sure, she hadn't been in every room, but she had been in the rooms he would likely frequent most.

Plus, there was the size of this house. He was one guy, with a townhouse in Chicago city. This place must be in the millions. Who could afford that on a doctor's salary? She couldn't. She was barely affording the smelliest apartment in the city.

'What did you have in the ER tonight?'

He paused, and then put his fork down for a moment. 'Stephen Bennett came back.'

'The guy with the chest tumour and the Horner's syndrome?'

Liam nodded. 'I think he was disappointed I was on duty. He wanted a second opinion.'

'Wow, what did you do?'

'I took him to the relatives' room to talk. I showed him his chest X-ray again, his blood tests, and explained the results. His biopsy result isn't through yet, but the oncologist I referred him to is sure it's cancerous.

'I told him he's free to go to any other hospital in the area. He can take a copy of his tests. He can speak to any doctor that he likes.'

She reached over and touched his hand. For a moment, it seemed like a buzz. The connection of his warm hand to her fingertips. She hadn't really meant anything by it, but now that she'd done it it seemed like so much more.

He was looking at her again. Those blue eyes

that watched like a laser in the ER seemed softer in the warm lights of his kitchen. Although the kitchen was modern, sleek and shiny, the Tiffany-style drop-down lampshade above them, accompanied by a matching small lamp on the table near by, cast warm rainbow colours around them.

It made her catch her breath. It made her want this second to last so much longer. But she couldn't stay silent for long. She didn't want him to realise she was having these kinds of thoughts.

'So, years ago, if someone told you they wanted a second opinion, would you have been offended?'

She watched the echoes of memories on his face. 'Of course,' he admitted.

'And now, why weren't you?' she prompted.

He let out a slow breath as a smile formed on his face. 'I saw a young man who is potentially terrified of being told he has cancer. He wants it to be anything but that. And I know that it doesn't matter who he goes to, the diagnosis will be the same.' He put a hand on his chest. 'I will have no bearing on that. And this isn't about me, it's about my patient.'

His blue eyes met her gaze. 'He did ask for your name, by the way.'

'He did? But I'm not a specialist.'

Liam nodded. 'But you are someone who was there. So, if he comes back in…'

'I'll sit him down and talk to him.' Maggie

nodded. 'Are we assuming he doesn't have a supportive network around him?'

Liam nodded and took a sip of his wine. 'It's what I'm guessing. He came by himself.'

'Maybe he moved to Chicago for work? Maybe his family is back home, somewhere else.'

'Could be.'

They looked at each other for a second. Maggie was wondering how she might feel, alone in Chicago with no friends, getting a diagnosis like that. It would be overwhelming.

She could tell Liam was letting the same thoughts run through his head. But he'd been here a while. He did have a circle of friends. But was home for him still Ireland? It made her question his family connections again.

Should she really be so bold as to ask? She thought about the photo on the stairs again. 'What about you?' she asked. 'What brought you to Chicago from Ireland?'

Liam licked his lips for a few moments. 'I decided to get away once I'd completed my training. Ireland was too small for me,' he gave a half-hearted smile, 'and I wanted to see the world.'

Liar was the first thing she thought, but didn't say it out loud. She could have said those words out loud herself and they would have been mainly true, but she could tell from the expression in Liam's eyes that there was much more to this.

Maybe he'd followed his heart. Maybe he'd met

someone and moved to be with them. She obviously wasn't here now. If it was a matter of the heart, maybe he would never tell.

'And what about this place?' She spread her arms wide. 'This house is gorgeous.'

He took a bite of his pasta. 'Family windfall.' It came out with no hesitation. She waited, but he didn't explain how.

She looked around again at the arched windows over the back garden and cornicing in the ceilings above her. 'People have always told me to invest in property and land.' She raised her eyebrows at him. 'But you have to find a place you want to stay first.' She gave a little sigh, and when she looked up he was staring at her with those inquisitive eyes. Well, if Liam wasn't prepared to share, then neither was she.

It was so much easier to change the subject.

'Anything else interesting today?'

'A few frequent flyers. Horace, our homeless man, who comes in for a feed but always refuses a shower. He got some shoes today.'

'He didn't have shoes?'

'He did, but they were someone else's. They took them back, so he came to ask if there were any in Lost Property he could have.'

'And were there?'

'He is now the proud owner of shiny red baseball boots that are only one size too big.'

'Who left them behind?'

'Who knows?' shrugged Liam. 'And if they come back for them, they've gone to a worthy owner.'

'What are you going to do about Barclay tomorrow?'

'I'm hoping he will be fine, and I'm off tomorrow anyway, so I can keep an eye on him.'

'I suspect he might have you making him scrambled egg and some strips of steak.'

Liam pretended to look shocked. 'You think I'd pander to him?'

She leaned her head on her hand. 'I know when I was at the shelter the other night, I made scrambled egg for some of the old guys and girls. You know, the ones with no teeth? They loved it.'

He gave her an interested look. 'You're working at a shelter?'

'Just three hours a week.'

'Which one?'

'Pondbank. They seem a nice bunch, just overwhelmed, like most other shelters.'

'Did you tell them you're a doctor?'

She could tell by his tone he knew exactly what this would result in. She laid her head on the counter. 'Yes, so after I made the scrambled egg, I assisted monitoring a dog during a surgery, and I helped deliver a stuck puppy.'

Liam's eyes narrowed in a fun way. 'And did you dropper-feed that puppy later because it wouldn't latch on?'

She lifted her head barely an inch from the counter. Her *yes* was merely a whisper.

'You should have told them you were an accountant.'

'I know,' she admitted. Then she glanced at her watch and sat up straight. 'Is that the time? I need to go.'

Liam turned and looked at the clock on the wall. Maggie was already on her feet, looking for her coat. 'Can you get me a cab?'

He nodded as he picked up his phone. 'What's your address?' he asked.

She rattled it off as she gathered her bag and tied her trainers. She heard him speak in a low voice, and groan.

Then he put something into an app on his phone and made another tiny strangled sound.

'What is it?'

He closed his eyes, clearly looking guilty. 'My bad,' he said.

'Your bad what?'

'There was a game tonight. Everyone must have just come out. No cabs for the next,' he glanced at his phone, 'two and a half hours.'

Maggie felt her chest tightening. She could get the L, Chicago's elevated train service. But that would require a twenty-minute walk to her place at the other end. It didn't fill her with glee.

'Stay here.' Liam said the words so quickly she wasn't quite sure she had heard them.

But they just made her heart pound faster. 'I c-can't do that,' she stammered.

'You can.' His arm swept out. 'I have plenty of space.' He glanced at the stairs. 'And if you're uncomfortable being upstairs with me, I can sleep down here.'

'In the dog bed?'

He let out a nervous laugh. 'No, on the sofa. There's plenty of room.'

She looked down at her clothes. She had flung on a T-shirt and leggings this morning after he'd called. She hadn't even thought twice about what she was wearing. But now she felt grubby. She didn't want to feel like this all night.

'I didn't bring anything,' she said simply.

He turned and walked away through the kitchen. She was confused for a second, then realised he was going to his utility room where the washer and dryer were. He came back holding a large grey T-shirt and a pair of sweats. 'They'll be too big, but they're just washed. And the en suite upstairs should have a spare toothbrush and toothpaste in it.'

'For your unexpected guests?' she couldn't help but say.

'Occasionally I have friends who visit,' he said, then rolled his eyes at her. 'Contrary to what you might think, I do have friends, Maggie.'

'I didn't say you didn't,' she answered smartly,

holding her hands out for the bundle of clothes as she asked herself if she was losing her mind.

He pointed to the upstairs. 'There are two rooms to choose from. Go and pick your place then come back down and I'll make you a cup of tea.'

She'd actually agreed to stay at Liam Kelly's place. Even though they hated each other at work. No one would believe this.

But the thought—terrifying as it was—was nowhere near as terrifying as walking through her dark, poorly lit neighbourhood at night. She could do this.

'Okay, thanks,' she said, reaching the staircase and taking a breath to slow herself, so she wouldn't run upstairs.

She knew which room was his, so deliberately chose the bedroom furthest away. It had an airy smell that made her know the sheets were freshly laundered. It was painted in pale cream, with a light beige carpet, a large dresser and floor-length mirror, plus an en suite complete with a deep bath and thick towels. She checked under the sink, and sure enough there was a brand-new toothbrush and toothpaste, and some generic toiletries. It was actually possible to survive here.

She put down the things he'd given her, ran her hand over the bedding, and wished her apartment could be like this.

By the time she got downstairs he was boiling the kettle, had set out some biscuits and had turned the TV on in the sitting room.

'Okay?' he asked.

'Yes, thanks,' she said.

'I do have to warn you,' he said as he poured the boiling water.

Her heart gave a little patter. 'Warn me of what?'

'Even though there isn't a bed in the room, that won't stop Barclay. There is a chance he'll nudge in next to you overnight.'

'Just as long as it's just the dog.' The words came out of her mouth before she could even stop them, and she wasn't sure who was more shocked, him or her.

He gave a nervous laugh and held up the steaming cup towards her. 'How do you take your tea?'

CHAPTER FIVE

IT SEEMED THAT autumn in Chicago brought everyone to the ER. Whether it was a scrape, a head knock, a slip or trip, a punch, a stomach-ache, or unknown abdominal pain—Liam had seen them all.

He was beginning to wonder if there was an environmental health issue at one of the eating establishments with the amount of gastric issues they seemed to be seeing. But careful questioning didn't flag up any particular place, and it just seemed as if the world had norovirus and had forgotten how to wash their hands.

His record at the moment was twelve kids from one infants class at once, and he dreaded to think how the rest of the school was doing. He'd even asked one of his nurses to give them a call with some basic advice that could be sent out to parents.

Thankfully, Barclay had recovered from his own gastric episode but he'd been acting kind of strange. It seemed as though he realised that

Maggie had stayed—indeed he had crept into her bed in the middle of night, but Maggie hadn't raised any objections.

But since then Barclay had kept wandering into the bedroom and whining, sniffing around the entire bed as if she was missing and he was looking for her.

Making the offer to stay had been impetuous, and had been the right thing to do, as it was his fault there was no ride home. Maggie had already been on his brain. Of course, he was keeping an eye on his new employee, making sure she was up to scratch. And she did seem to be.

He was also making sure he had a few words ready every day to try and stump her with. But he was beginning to realise that Maggie Sullivan was every bit as competitive as he'd been with his brother and they might end up in a stand-off position. Not that any of the staff would complain, because it would just mean double the doughnuts. But Liam Kelly didn't like to lose.

The call came in just as most of the staff had started to contemplate lunch. As a level-one trauma centre, if there was any major emergency Williams Memorial would get the call.

The red phone ringing was such a rare phenomenon that it made everyone jump and its noise cast an eerie silence around the ER.

Liam took two long strides and answered it

before it rang twice. 'Williams Memorial, what have you got?'

He listened, asked a few questions, felt his skin chill and his stomach flip. He'd dealt with major incidents before. It was never pleasant. And the come-down after running on adrenaline for hours was even more exhausting. He could sense all eyes on him.

When he put down the phone, he pushed some things aside. 'A major incident has been declared at Midway International Airport. Multiple casualties. They are requesting a team, and want to know how many patients we can take.' He turned to one of his charge nurses. 'Mhairi, you're on point. Dr Nduji, you will be in charge of triage. Clear as many cubicles as possible and phone the bed manager to find out how much space we have. Call in all staff currently off duty.' He pointed to one of the admin staff. 'Page Surgical, Vascular, Neurology and Anaesthetics.' Maggie had just appeared beside him. 'Maggie and I will go out with Jem, Lisa and Frank. We will send back as much information as we can.' He put his hands on his hips and took a breath. 'Any questions, ask me in the next few minutes—after that we'll be on site.'

Staff had pulled their phones from their pockets to check social media for information on an 'incident' at Midway Airport. A call came in from the fire and rescue crew, letting them know they would pick up the medical teams en route.

Liam took Maggie and the rest of the team to a cupboard where all the gear they would need was stored. They put on jackets with their designations and slung the rucksacks over their shoulders.

As they moved outside to wait for the fire and rescue trucks, Jem handed her phone to Liam. It was an aircraft. On fire.

He took a breath, and told himself they could do this. A few people ran up to ask him questions that he answered quickly. The fire and rescue trucks pulled up, lights flashing, and they climbed in.

'Any more news?' he asked as they took off.

'Crash landing. One aircraft. Haven't yet been told how many people were on board, just news of multiple casualties. Three level-one centres have been activated.'

Liam nodded. It was normal for more than one hospital to be alerted in an event like this. Intensive care units were small and could be easily overwhelmed with victims from one event. It was better to spread the load across a number of hospitals to ensure all patients received the care that they should.

They couldn't really speak in the truck, as the sirens were blaring, but after a few moments a hand slid into his. Maggie's. Was she worried?

Maybe he was taking her to something she wasn't ready for?

He glanced down at her as he squeezed her hand. A further look let him know that she was also holding Jem's hand at the other side. Jem looked as if she might be sick. Liam's stomach flipped again. He'd just gathered the staff he thought might be best equipped to deal with this. But he hadn't actually asked any of them if they would do it. There was just an assumption about healthcare staff. And now he thought about it, that was wrong. Sadly, in certain professions, you sometimes had to deal with things that others might never have to face. It was part of the job. But he'd still made assumptions he would have to consider later.

He moved his other hand over Maggie's. Her fingers were cold. His brain was still ticking over with what they might find when they got there. At least it was still daylight. They wouldn't be tackling multiple casualties at night. That would make things ten times worse.

The journey was quick. Sometimes, unbelievably, traffic got in the way of emergency vehicles—as if they thought their journey was more important. But today it was clear. Everyone was listening to the news on the radio. Cars, trucks and buses were all pulling over to clear the way for the emergency vehicles.

Liam pressed his face up to the window, wondering when he would actually see something. The radio started squawking. It addressed their fire truck. 'Fire truck 51, come to the west exit and take the right runway. All airport traffic has ceased. You are clear to proceed. Fire truck 43 is ahead of you.'

Even from inside the fire truck, it was the noise Liam heard first. The whoosh of the flames.

He'd never been exposed to fires before. Not like these guys had. They had their equipment on in seconds, and they jumped down, donning their masks and gear, and connecting and releasing the hoses. There was a shout. A clear order for them to stay back right now. And, while Liam wanted to rush ahead to see if there was anything he could do to help, the last thing he wanted was to get in their way. They knew what they were doing.

The aircraft was in pieces. Parts of the fuselage were burning brightly. The smell of oil in the air was acrid. Debris seemed to litter the runway and Liam couldn't really tell where it started.

There was a shout to their right, and Liam saw some other medical staff from another hospital waving them over.

He gave the signal to his team and took off at a run. A man in a jacket that read Team Lead pointed to a number of people lying on the ground. 'Start here, please. Triage—we've no central point right now, and the firefighters are just bringing us whoever they find.'

'They don't need assistance on site?'

The guy shook his head. 'We've been told to keep clear.'

Liam nodded and fell to his knees on the ground next to an older man. He had an obvious head injury, a broken shoulder and was short of breath. Maggie tended to a woman on his other side, who was pale, shaking and had burns to some of her extremities.

Liam tied a tag on the man, recorded his Glasgow coma scale, bandaged his head, put his arm in a temporary sling and sounded his chest. 'Transfer to a receiving unit,' he said to the EMT who came up behind him, and moved next to Maggie.

It was difficult to deal with burns in the field. Maggie had already started a wide-bore IV. People who were burned generally lost lots of fluid, so had to be kept topped up. 'Administer some morphine?'

She nodded. 'Please.'

Morphine was a controlled drug. In the hospital it was kept in a locked cupboard and two members of staff had to sign for any usage. In the field, there were still rules. Liam pulled out an ampule, let Maggie see it, and drew up the drug. Burns were extremely painful, and this was the most effective pain relief that they had. He administered and they both initialled. He recorded it on the tag that had been placed around the woman's arm and they handed her over to the next ambulance that arrived.

People were being brought over all the time. Some were carried by fire crew, and some stumbled over on their own. Many were upset and disorientated. Some were looking for family members.

Jem ended up alongside one of the police officers, checking people over quickly and making sure nothing was missed, before allowing some of the people to go along to a makeshift waiting area.

Lisa and Frank worked alongside Maggie and Liam, pulling things from the packs instantly, checking blood pressure, applying wound covers, hanging IVs, noting patient details and keeping everything running smoothly.

'Kid!' came the shout, and the next second Liam heard pounding footsteps.

There was no time to think. Lisa laid out a sterile blanket just as a child with burns was laid down in front of them. She wasn't crying but her eyes were wide with fear and she was shaking uncontrollably.

'Cut what you can,' said Liam, knowing that some of the clothing fabric might adhere to the burns. They would take away what they could, without causing damage. Some of this might need to be done in a theatre. 'Maggie, some pain relief.'

They looked at each other. Calculating weights in their head. '2.5 mg?'

Liam nodded at her approximation as he slid a wide-bore IV into the only vein he could find. This child was shutting down fast.

'Do we have any information on this kid?' he asked. 'Name? Underlying conditions?'

Lisa made a noise. 'There's an insulin pump under her top.'

'Is it functioning?'

Lisa held up her hands. It was clear she had no idea.

'Can we get a blood-sugar level?' Liam felt a wave of panic. 'Does anyone know what heat might do to an insulin pump…is there a chance it can malfunction?'

Blank faces stared back. 'Disconnect it,' said Maggie. 'If we don't know, we can't risk it. There's too much else at play here.' She was looking down at some of the burns that were clearly dirty and would be at a high risk of infection.

'Her airway is swelling,' said Maggie as she listened to the girl's chest.

'Is there an anaesthetist here?' shouted Liam.

A medic he didn't recognise from another hospital came over. 'Can you prioritise this kid? In shock, first-degree burns in some areas, also type 1 diabetic. We've disconnected the pump until you can get things stabilised here. Wide-bore IV in place, airway swelling, 2.5 mg morphine administered and no ID.'

The anaesthetist went straight to work, calling one of his staff over. Within minutes the little girl was sedated, intubated and covered in another sterile sheet, and the team would try to deal with the rest of burns on the way to hospital.

'Liam!' Maggie gave a quiet shout to where she'd moved on to deal with a woman dressed in a cabin-crew uniform. Her face was covered in soot, she had some burns to her hands and forearms, but Maggie was checking her head.

She spoke in a calm voice. 'Can you tell me your name?'

Words came out, but they didn't make sense.

'I'm going to put some gel on your hands and arms to cover them until we get you to hospital. Are you having any trouble breathing?'

The woman looked confused. She tilted her head, wincing as Maggie gently touched her with hand with sterile gloves, and spoke again, not making any sense.

Maggie stood up, walking around her patient and checking her head and neck from all angles. 'I'm not finding any injury,' she said, frowning. She ran her hands over the woman's scalp, trying to feel for any lumps or bumps.

'What airline is this?' Although he was sure this woman was confused, Liam didn't want to be an idiot and find out later that the woman simply spoke another language.

Maggie pointed to the uniform. 'This is a US airline,' she said. 'I'd expect her to be able to speak English.'

She pulled out her pen torch and checked the woman's pupils.

'Anything?' asked Liam.

'Right is slightly sluggish.' She took a breath. 'I think we should prioritise her potential head injury and confusion over her other injuries.'

Liam nodded. 'Agreed.' He looked over to Frank. 'Can you arrange for immediate transport?'

Frank disappeared. He was ex-military and the calmest man on the planet in an emergency. Liam didn't think he'd ever seen him break sweat. He came back a few minutes later, swept the woman up into his arms as if she didn't weigh anything. 'Her tag updated?' he checked with Maggie.

Maggie nodded, and Frank disappeared into the throng of people.

'Hey guys, over here!'

It was a shout from one of the fire crew. He jogged over. 'I need you over here.'

Maggie and Liam picked up their packs and ran. What they saw next took them a few moments to compute in their brains. Lisa, who was behind them, summed things up. 'Wow,' she said simply.

There were two people, still strapped into their seats, sitting to the side of the runway. It was as though someone had picked up this piece of the plane and just dropped it here. Both people seemed to be unconscious.

The firefighter held up his hands at their stunned faces. 'Questions later. Can you check these two and establish if they are safe to move?'

'Of course,' said Liam as he nodded at Maggie and knelt beside one of the patients. Maggie knelt by the other. They spoke in quiet voices, trying to rouse their patients, checking for vital signs. Maggie's patient let out a groan and started to thrash around in confusion for a moment. Liam's patient stayed very quiet. He gave Maggie a stare that spoke a thousand words. It was likely this elderly man and woman had been travelling together, but they didn't want to make assumptions. He held his fingers gently at the man's wrist, assuring himself of what he already knew.

The woman was now more vocal, though had no idea what had happened. 'What's your name?' Maggie asked.

'Linda,' she managed. Then she furrowed her brow. 'Am I in Scotland? How did that happen?'

Maggie gave a soft laugh and put her hand on the woman's arm. 'You're not in Scotland. You're in Chicago. I'm a doctor. Can you tell me if anything hurts?'

Linda took a moment to think. 'Well, everything hurts, but not really.'

Liam saw Maggie give her a wide smile. 'Just like normal, then?'

Linda nodded. 'Just like normal.'

Maggie started running her hands up and down Linda's legs, gently examining her abdomen and pelvis, then checking her back too. 'I just need to be sure that nothing is broken before we move you, Linda.' She gave a nod to Lisa. 'Can you see if we can find a wheelchair?'

Maggie kept talking, and it was clear she was trying to keep Linda distracted. Once Lisa appeared with the wheelchair, she nodded towards it. 'We're going to help you into this, and then Lisa will take you to be checked over further. Is that your husband you were travelling with?'

Liam's heart could have broken in that second as he saw the recognition dawn on Linda's face. Her head whipped around towards him. 'Ben? Is he okay?' She reached her free hand over and tapped Ben on the arm. 'Honey, wake up, wake up.'

Liam gave her a soft smile. 'Let me take care of Ben. You go with Lisa right now.'

Linda was clearly still disorientated from the events. 'Am I in Ireland?' she asked.

Liam kept his smile on his face. 'I'm visiting. Don't worry, you're in Chicago.'

There were only a few tiny scrapes on her

arms and a graze on her face. Other than that, she seemed fine, and Maggie moved her into the chair that Lisa brought over, and watched as she was wheeled away.

Frank appeared back next to them. 'What do you need? A gurney?' He looked at Ben and clearly realised that he was dead. He put a hand on Liam's shoulder. 'Let me find out what we do here. I heard one of the police chiefs talk about a crime scene. I'm not sure if we will be able to move him.'

Liam nodded as Frank walked away. 'I'm not leaving him here,' he said simply to Maggie. 'I won't leave a dead man sitting in his aeroplane seat out in the open.'

'What do you think happened to him?'

He gave a sorry look at Ben. 'There's no obvious trauma. Just like with Linda. But he could have had a stroke, a heart attack, or maybe it's just plain shock. Can you imagine what their bodies have gone through?'

'Do we even know what happened yet?' She stared around at the scene in front of them. 'This part seems impossible. Two people, still in their seats, far away from the rest of the aircraft. Someone will need to spell this out to me.'

Liam pulled a tag from his pack and started writing Ben's details on it. 'I'm going to go and see if we can get someone to contact the family.

I'm not sure about telling Linda that Ben is dead without her having some family support.'

Maggie ran her hands through her hair, which was starting to unravel from its clasp. 'I'm still worried about her. There was no obvious sign of trauma, but what if half her bones have shattered from the impact, and the force of their seats being thrown over here? What if her whole body is running on adrenaline right now, and she's just not feeling any pain?'

Liam nodded thoughtfully. Frank was in the distance, pulling a gurney that looked as if it had come from one of the ambulances. 'Why don't you go and check on her again? I'll deal with Ben, and then see if there is anyone else to treat.'

Maggie finished tying up her hair again. He could see something in her eyes. 'That kid,' she murmured. 'That little kid with the burns. We don't even know her name.'

Instinctively, Liam reached out and grabbed her, pulling her into a hug. For him, it was natural. And he knew these days that some people would frown upon it. But Liam had always acted on his natural instincts, and had yet to be proven wrong.

From staff members, to patients, to relatives, human touch could be so important, and sometimes the moment called for it.

He could feel Maggie take a few shuddery breaths against his chest. Her arms were wrapped around his waist, and he rubbed her back gently. 'We can follow her up too. Right now, it's just what we do at the scene—smash and grab, and treat if we can. We don't have to like this.'

She nodded, her head against his chest. They were here to try and assess people and save as many lives as they could. Magic hour or golden hour—that was the time period they were in, that first hour where interventions could be the difference between a patient living or dying.

He stayed like that for a few moments, feeling the rise and fall of their chests together. He knew Maggie had come to Chicago alone. She didn't have a support system in place around her, and he was suddenly conscious of the fact he could be doing more to help her.

But were his motives pure? He couldn't even consider that right now. Not while they were at the scene of a major incident. All he knew was, he wouldn't let her go home tonight without talking to her first.

Frank came over, completely unperturbed by seeing Liam hugging Maggie. 'I didn't like what they told me, so I improvised.'

Maggie lifted her head but didn't immediately move from her position. 'What did they say?'

'They actually started having an argument with each other. Something about who should be in charge of the investigation.'

'Who were they?'

Frank shrugged. ‘Police guy and airport guy. So, I figured we’ll just take Ben back to Williams and go from there. They can sort it out later.’

Liam gave a nod and reluctantly stepped back from Maggie. She seemed to collect herself and straightened up. ‘I’ll go and check on Linda again.’ She picked up her pack and disappeared.

Liam helped Frank lift Ben onto the gurney and quickly checked to see if there were any belongings around him, but there were none. Frank tucked a blanket around Ben, and they pushed the gurney back to where ambulances were gathered. Obviously, they didn’t want to potentially use an ambulance required by injured patients, but a police officer near by seemed to understand what was required. ‘Hi, guys, you got details?’

Liam nodded and pointed to the tag. ‘Perfect, let me deal with things for you, then. Any request as to where the gentleman goes?’

Frank tapped the guy on the shoulder. ‘Williams if you can.’

‘No problem, Corporal,’ he replied.

Liam raised his eyebrows. Frank gave a nod of his head for them to head back to the field. ‘We served together. If you want something done, ask an army man. Let the rest of them fight about it.’

Liam smiled and adjusted his pack again on his shoulders. ‘Let’s go and see where we can be useful.’

* * *

Maggie was jittery. Not because of anything she'd seen or experienced in the last few hours, but because she was cold, and hadn't eaten in hours.

She still couldn't fathom what had actually happened here. She kept having to step over shards of twisted metal, and the smell of aviation fuel was still apparent, even though the whole area had been doused in foam.

She'd patched multiple minor injuries. Most of the people, travellers and airline staff, were in some form of shock. She'd no idea of the number of fatalities. She just knew she'd seen more burns and smoke inhalation than she'd ever wanted to.

Apparently the first few crews on site had mainly dealt with traumatic injuries. Some amputations, some penetrating wounds made by bits of the aircraft.

She'd heard numerous theories in the last hour. There had been something on the runway that collided with a plane ready to take off. There was something on the runway that collided with a plane that had landed. There had been an explosion on an aeroplane just about to take off, or land. An engine had exploded on landing, ripping through the plane and causing all the destruction.

Maggie had absolutely no expertise in planes. She didn't know which runways were used for taking off, or landing, so couldn't differentiate between any of those things.

She just continued to assess any patient she was asked to see. Someone handed her a bar of chocolate at one point as she had just finished listening to a patient's chest. 'You look like you could pass out,' a firefighter said to her under his breath.

'Thanks,' she said, eating the bar in two giant bites, and continuing to do what needed to be done.

'Is there a doctor available?' came a shout.

'Yes!' she replied, jumping up with her pack. Liam had replied too, but the firefighter in charge looked over them both. 'I'll take the skinny one,' he said, pointing to her.

Liam went to open his mouth, but she was already running alongside the man, moving to a pile of twisted metal that she couldn't even decipher what it had once been.

'Stand there,' one of the firefighters instructed. 'Hold your breath and turn your head away.'

A few seconds later, she was doused in foam.

'How are you with small spaces?' The main firefighter was back in front of her.

'Fine,' she said. 'What do you need?'

'I've got a girl trapped in there. I need you to figure out a way for us to get her out safely.'

He handed her a pair of safety goggles and guided her towards a gap in the twisted metal. There was a hand extended towards her.

She didn't think too much and just took it.

The hand pulled her inside. 'Tuck in your elbows,' came the instruction. She did as she was told, took a few seconds to get her bearings within the distorted structure and slid off her jacket. No wonder the firefighter had picked her instead of Liam. No way would those broad shoulders get in this small space.

The firefighter to her left pointed forward. 'We've got a young woman…she's pinned, and we need to know if we can remove the metal.'

Maggie stuck her head through the mangled frame. She could see the blonde-haired young woman, who was barely conscious. Her shoulder was speared with a large, jagged shard of metal, keeping her in place next to a part of the plane. Maggie tilted her head to the side, trying to work out what she was looking at. A seat was upside down above her, which was totally disorientating. Although Maggie was crouching right now, her feet were actually on the inside roof of the plane. Maggie made a grab for her stethoscope and tried to listen to the girl's chest. Her colour was deathly pale with a hint of blue. From listening it was clear that one of her lungs had collapsed due to the penetrating injury.

'Do we have a name?' she asked.

'She's not been conscious long enough. We heard her screaming earlier—that's how we found her—but we've not been able to get in properly.

We can't bring our normal cutting equipment because of the risk of igniting the aviation fuel.'

'Even if we cover the whole thing in foam?'

The guy shook his head. 'Still too dangerous.'

There was literally no room to move. There was no way to get a chest tube in position. She turned to the man behind her. 'Ask the other doctor, Liam, to get ready for an emergency chest intubation. We need oxygen ready. Can you tell him I think she's probably got a haemothorax instead of a pneumothorax, and she's probably going to lose a lot of blood.'

The firefighter's eyes widened. 'How do you want to do this?'

'Honestly? I want us to do this in under ten seconds. I'm going to inject her with some local anaesthetic around the site.' She spoke under her breath. 'Not that I think it will make any real difference. But it's something. I can't risk morphine at this stage. We're going to get that shard of metal out, move her as quickly as possible, and let Liam do what he needs to do when she's outside.'

The firefighter gave her a careful glance. 'You don't want to try and do this slowly?'

'There's no time. I suspect she's bleeding internally already.' She lowered her voice. 'I think this lady could bleed to death. Let's do this now.'

Her voice was steady. But steady was the last thing Maggie was feeling right now. She didn't care about the twisted metal around them. She didn't care about the restricted space. All she cared about was removing the metal that was pinning the girl, and yanking her out.

She spoke in a quiet voice to the firefighter. 'I'm pretty sure her lung is full of blood. She's going to bleed from that shoulder wound as soon as we remove the metal—and there is a chance it could have penetrated an artery. Speed is all that matters. As soon as the metal is out, we need to get her through this structure and out to where she can be treated.'

Maggie grabbed the local anaesthetic and injected it around the metal shard. It was awkward and difficult to try and position herself to get to all points in the wound. The young lady didn't flinch. This was awful. If they left her, she would bleed to death and die. If they moved her, there was still every chance she could still bleed to death and die.

'Doc, your man is outside. He says he's ready when you are.'

Maggie took a few breaths. Trust. It was the thing that flooded over her. She trusted that if she got this girl out, she would have the best chance possible if Liam was treating her.

She looked at the firefighter. 'Ready?' He nodded. 'Then pull!'

The noise of the metal being pulled from the flesh, followed by the young woman's scream would stay with Maggie forever. As soon as the woman was freed her body slumped over and Maggie tried to stem the bleeding.

A firefighter was pulling at the young woman's feet…it would be the only way to get her out of here. Her body started sliding through the slim space, Maggie still keeping track and holding a pad in place while she could.

A few seconds later, the woman was past her completely and she could hear Liam's voice outside.

Maggie couldn't just jump out—she had to twist herself and tilt her hips to get back through the carcass of metal. The firefighter was right behind her. Neither of them wanted to stay in here any longer than necessary.

As her feet hit the ground outside, she could see Liam already had a tube in place. It was filled with blood—just as she suspected. Frank was there, squeezing a bag of IV fluids in, to try and keep the woman's levels up. Maggie turned to the firefighter clambering out behind her. 'Any identifying belongings?'

He shook his head. 'We know she was tossed out of her seat. There's just no way to tell. We can't even check the manifest, because we don't know what seat she was in.'

Maggie moved next to Liam. 'What do you need?'

'Patch the shoulder,' he said, still working with the vacuum seal on the drain.

Maggie dug in her pack for the wound dressing—similar to those used in combat because they were effective at patching wounds and stopped blood loss. It took her less than twenty seconds to apply.

Frank nodded underneath the gurney, and she saw the oxygen cylinder, turning it on and putting the mask on the woman's face. She lifted the portable monitor and attached leads to anywhere she could find free skin on the woman's chest, and switched it on.

Two EMTs appeared at their sides. 'Are you ready?'

'Are there more patients?' asked Liam.

One of the firefighters spoke. 'I think all the majors are handled.'

'In that case, I'll go back with her.'

Maggie watched as Liam hurried alongside the gurney as it was wheeled across the tarmac towards a waiting ambulance.

'Better get that stitched,' said someone to her side.

She looked down. There was a large bleeding gash on her forearm. It had obviously happened as she'd squeezed through the metal carcass. She hadn't even felt it. She picked up her jacket from the ground, and looked for her backpack. 'I've got it!' yelled Frank. 'Come on and I'll blag us a ride back to Memorial.'

Maggie looked out across the tarmac. It was still a scene of destruction. How they would get this back to a functioning airport she had no idea.

But she knew they would. This was just how people like her worked. Her arm started to sting as she walked back to where everyone was gathering. She'd never felt tiredness like it. She couldn't wait to get back to the hospital. Familiar surroundings. People she knew.

Maggie almost stumbled over her own feet. For the first time since she'd got here, Chicago was actually starting to feel like home.

CHAPTER SIX

THE ER WAS BUSY, but calm. They cleared Resus and Liam took the young lady straight through. A chest X-ray confirmed the position of the tube and her injuries to the chest area. He was able to give her some pain relief, and she finally started to come around.

By the time she was handed over to the ICU staff, they still didn't have an ID for her, but one of the airport staff would check the passports scanned there to match her.

He could smell coffee and pizza, and wanted both instantly.

He took a quick walk around the department, making sure everyone knew what they were doing, and there were no queries. It wasn't just hospital staff—there were also EMTs, firefighters, police, and all knew they were welcome, so by the time he made it to the staff room there was barely any space left.

But it only took him an instant to spot her. Maggie was sitting on a chair, a kind of vacant look on her face. Her arm was resting on a sterile pack, and he could see a clear dressing covering a wound that clearly needed to be stitched.

He looked around, grabbed two coffees, piled sugar into one, and took two slices of pizza and some napkins. He dropped into the seat next to her and handed over the coffee, sitting her pizza on top of her sterile pack.

'I'll ask you about that once you've eaten and had something to drink.'

At some point, she'd lost her clasp and her hair had tumbled all around her face. It was longer than he'd expected, and his first thought was how pretty she was with it down.

Maggie was just sitting, breathing slowly, so he gave her a nudge. He kept his voice low. 'Are you okay…do you need something?'

She gave a little shudder and turned to look at him. 'No, I'm fine.' She glanced down at the coffee and pizza. 'Thanks for this.'

'Well, eat. I think it's too busy for us to do a debrief today, so I'll just chat to folks at the end of their shift and do the debrief tomorrow.'

She'd taken a sip of her coffee and winced for a moment, clearly reacting to the sugar, but continued to drink. 'No, do it this evening. A lot of staff were called in. Most of them might not be around tomorrow. Plus, you don't know where people's minds might go tonight. Do it soon.'

Liam could feel the tension knotting his body

again. He knew she was right. But after running on adrenaline for the last few hours, he really wanted some downtime. ‘Okay,’ he said simply as she started to eat the pizza.

They stayed in the staff room for another ten minutes, finishing their pizza and coffee. ‘Right,’ he said, pointing at her arm, ‘let’s get this sorted.’

She gave a sigh and followed him through to one of the cubicles. Liam set up a dressing pack, cleaned her wound, injected her with some local and started stitching. ‘You’ll need to keep an eye on this. Any pain, redness, swelling, tell me and I’ll put you on some antibiotics…we just don’t know what might have been on that metal. Are your normal vaccinations up-to-date?’

She nodded, then pulled a face as her phone sounded. ‘Sorry, I meant to turn that off.’

Liam pointed to the screen, where he could see multiple messages. ‘What’s going on?’

Maggie closed her eyes as he continued to stitch. ‘It’s my landlord. The apartment…well, it stinks. It’s mouldy. There’s clearly wet or damp somewhere. I swear the smell is starting to permeate my pores.’

He looked up from cutting his final stitch. ‘And?’

She let out a slow breath. ‘It’s the last thing I need today. I complained. He’d been ignoring my messages since I got here. I started looking for somewhere else, but he insists I pay the whole lease. And now he's telling me to get out.'

Liam placed a clean dressing on her wound. 'He what?'

'I reported him to the landlords' association. He found out,' she waved a hand, 'and I haven't even read all the stuff that he's made up to say I'm a bad tenant.' She gave Liam a sad smile. 'We haven't exactly had time for that today, you know.' She held up one hand. 'Priorities.'

He could see everything on her face. Her tiredness, which matched his. The stress of the day. The strain of living somewhere she was clearly unhappy with and having to navigate the laws and rules in Chicago. The fact she had no real support systems around her.

It wasn't his job. It wasn't his role. But he wanted to wrap her up in a hug and tell her everything would be okay. He wanted to offer to kick the landlord's ass.

Even just the thought of how she'd been treated made his blood boil. 'Who is this guy?' he asked. 'Does he have any idea of the kind of day we've all had, and he's threatening to throw you out today? Is he online? Chicago people won't take kindly to a landlord throwing out a doctor who's spent her day saving lives at the airport.'

Maggie gave him another tired smile. 'Let me deal with it. To be honest, I want out. I hate the thought of any of my belongings smelling like that place. I can find a hotel to stay in tonight and try and sort things out tomorrow.'

She touched the dressing. 'Thanks for this. Now, let's go and do the debrief. We need to tell everyone just what a good job they've done today.'

She straightened her shoulders, her head coming up and the expression on her face changing. Maggie could be like a chameleon when she needed to. Even though he knew just how exhausted she was right now, it was clear this was her face for her colleagues: pride, assurance and perfectly on point.

He admired that. After the day they'd had, what they'd seen, he admired that she wanted to put her colleagues first.

But the thing was, he wanted to tell his staff too how proud he was of them. Maybe she was starting to rub off on him?

When he blinked he could remember the faces of his staff on site. How he'd watched things flit across their eyes, then clearly been put away so they could do their job. And Frank had been remarkable. His army training had shone through.

Liam moved to the centre of the nurses' station, where most staff tended to collect. He stood up on a chair so that he could be seen. 'Everyone, if you have time, gather round. We want to do a debrief for everyone before people start going home.'

One of the admin staff handed him a sheet of

info he'd asked her to pull together when they got back. Even looking at the numbers now made him take a breath.

People started to gather around him, and not just the ER hospital staff. There were firefighters, EMTs, police officers and staff from other departments.

'I just want to say a huge thank you to everyone who came to assist today. The team at the airport and everyone back here has done a tremendous job.' He took a minute. 'We all deal with difficult cases. We still don't know the real circumstances of what happened today. But we do know there were two hundred and twelve passengers and eight crew on board.'

He let the numbers settle with the staff. 'Ourselves, St Matthew's, and Pennington General were the level-one trauma centres responding. We've had eighty-three patients through our doors. Forty-one are currently admitted or receiving treatment. I'd like to remind you that not all of our patients are identified yet. We may still have relatives trying to find family members, and patients looking for people they were travelling with.'

Liam looked up at a man and woman in the corner. 'Leah and Anjar are co-ordinating all enquiries, please go to them first or direct any family members to them, so we are sure that people are getting the correct information.'

He could see the staff members exchanging glances and nodding at each other. 'I know that going home after a day like this is hard. I want to remind you that we are all human. And I'll say the last thing you expect me to. This is just a job. If you've found today hard, come and talk to me, or Jo, our staff counsellor. If you need some time off, you can say that. If you want to follow up on some of the patients you've treated, then please do. Sometimes we find that patients involved in traumatic situations relate best to the person who treated them first. Equally, if that's something you would find difficult, that's fine. I want you all to go home tonight being proud of the job that you did. If you want to talk about systems and processes and can think of any way we can do things better, then please know we want to hear it. Come and have those chats whenever you're ready. But most of all, go home, relax and hug those that you love the most. Call the people whose voices you want to hear. Know that after a major incident, some people struggle to sleep. It's the adrenaline, and it can be a,' he gave a wide smile to everyone, 'if you're from Ireland or Scotland,' he nodded at Maggie, 'a bugger.'

There was a ripple of laughter amongst the staff. Most of them had heard Liam's expressions before.

'Please, people, go home and relax. Let me

know if you need anything from me and again, thank you all.'

He jumped down and took another breath. Maggie put her hand on his arm. 'Well done.'

He nodded. 'You were right. I had to do it tonight. I just hope our staff are going to be okay. I can't possibly know what they all saw, or had to deal with.'

Her phone beeped again and he raised his eyebrows. She shook her head. 'I'm not even looking. I don't have the energy.'

'I brought my car today. Why don't I drop you off, rather than you take the L?'

He saw the tiny flash of worry on her face that passed in an instant. She sighed. 'You know what? That would be great.'

They picked up their stuff and headed to Liam's car. 'Nice wheels,' she commented as they got in, and he headed out into the traffic.

It was dark by the time they reached her neighbourhood and Maggie gave him some directions until they were practically at her front door.

He switched the engine off and looked at her. 'I'm walking you to the door.'

She started to object but he held up his hand. 'If you start, I'll just phone my mother and set her on you. If she heard I'd let you walk to the apartment yourself in the dark, she'd be on the next flight over from Ireland.'

As the words left his lips, his brain instantly

flew back to the airport. It was clear Maggie's had too, and they just breathed for a few moments in silence.

'Okay,' she finally said and opened the car door.

The building that housed her apartment had a key fob entrance and as soon as they climbed the stairs, he could see Maggie stiffen.

There was an angry note taped to the front of her door:

BE OUT BY TOMORROW

Maggie started to shake and Liam ripped the note from the door. 'He can't do that. Who does he think he is?'

She kept her head low and opened the door.

As they stepped inside, he felt the slight chill in the air, and the aroma. It was either damp or mould, or a mixture of both. It was definitely unpleasant.

'Let's pack up your things.'

Maggie was standing in the kitchen; she seemed almost frozen.

He put a hand on her shoulder. 'Maggie?'

She looked up at him, and he could see the tears threatening to spill down her face, and knew she was fighting with every cell in her body to stop that happening.

It was as though her brain was full of thoughts and feelings that just didn't have anywhere to go.

She stared around at the contents of her apartment and swallowed, clearly trying to take things in.

'Maggie,' he said firmly. 'Pack. I don't like the attitude of this guy, and I don't want you to be here by yourself in case he comes back. Pack now, and I'll help you get moved.'

She pulled out her phone. 'I'll need to find somewhere; I'll need to book a hotel.'

'You don't need to do that. You can stay with me.'

She stopped dead and looked up at him. 'What?' And then, 'I can't do that.'

'You can, and you will.'

'But…'

'But nothing. This place smells terrible—no wonder you were complaining. Pack up your clothes, tell me what else is yours and I'll pack it for you, and we'll get out of here.'

She looked as if she wanted to argue again, but he watched as she lifted her head, visibly sniffed the air, and wrinkled her nose. 'I hate this place,' she said, and a determined smile appeared on her face.

She pointed to two kitchen units. 'I have bags under the kitchen sink. Can you empty the cupboards and the fridge?' He nodded and got to work.

Maggie packed her suitcases in record time and pulled them towards the door, along with a heap of bedsheets. 'I'm going to just dump these. I worry the smell will never leave them, and you'll let me use yours, won't you?'

She gave him a cheeky wink.

'How did you pack those cases so quickly?'

'Because I packed without any care and attention, because I'll need to wash the whole lot to get rid of any potential smell. You do have a washer and dryer, don't you?'

'It's all yours,' he sighed, 'but you are going to have to explain some of the food in your cupboards.'

'What do you mean?' She peered in the bags he was holding. 'You lived in Ireland—you must know all these brands.' She looked up at him. 'It's just baked beans and chocolate biscuits.'

'Not exactly the main food groups.'

She shrugged. 'We can debate that.'

He gathered up some books she pointed out to him and carried everything to his car. 'Are you sure that's everything?'

She nodded. 'I still have stuff in New York in storage. I hadn't shipped it, because as soon as I arrived and smelled the place I knew I didn't want to stay there long. So I was really just surviving with what I arrived with.'

He drove them through the city, as Maggie sat with the keys in her hands. 'I will start looking for somewhere else. I absolutely appreciate this is just a temporary measure.'

It was a get-out clause. And he knew it. She

was wondering if he was regretting his offer. Maybe she was worried he hadn't really meant it.

But he had. Could there be an ulterior motive? Maybe. He wasn't sure. He liked Maggie Sullivan. Actually, more than liked.

But he didn't want to step over a line.

'Did I say this was a temporary offer? I mean, I know you're house-trained and my dog likes you.'

She gave a nervous laugh. 'I stayed one night. Living with someone is entirely different.'

'You know that?'

The air between them seemed to still. He saw the expression on her face, and turned his own back to the road.

After a few moments' pause she answered. 'I do know that, but actually I don't know anything.'

'What does that mean?'

She let out a sigh, and ran her hands through her hair. 'I was dating someone in New York.'

'And?'

'And my observation and assessment skills are clearly lacking.'

He gave a half-laugh. 'What does that mean?'

'It means I dated someone for eighteen months, was ready to move into an apartment with them, and his wife turned up on my doorstep.'

The car halted, and Liam pointed ahead. 'I'm glad this is a red light. Because…what?'

She shook her head and let out a long breath.

'I know, I'm a fool, and now I think back—yes, they were signs, but because I wasn't looking for them, I didn't see them.'

'But that's not on you, that's on him.'

She raised her eyebrows. 'Really?'

'Well, he clearly lied to you.'

'Yes, he did. But I should have spotted something, I should have realised. It shouldn't have taken… Marjory turning up at my doorstep for the penny to finally drop.'

'Marjory?' It came out as a bit of a laugh.

'Yeah, kind of old-fashioned name. Funnily enough, I didn't feel the urge to ask why, or why she had a husband who dared to cheat on her.'

'What did you say to him?'

There was silence. He waited until they'd pulled away again before he shot a glance at her.

'Maggie?'

She pulled a face.

'You didn't?'

She still didn't answer.

'Tell me you said something to him.'

She let the silence hang, then eventually said, 'Well, I did some other stuff.'

'Spray-paint his car, get him parking tickets, complain to his employer about something, put him on a dating site?'

She held up her hands. 'All reasonable options. I'll keep them in mind for the future.'

'Maggie, what did you do?'

'I came here.'

'What?'

'I blocked him, packed up, and came here.'

He wrinkled his nose, trying to get his head around this. 'You didn't find him and yell at him?' He lowered his voice. 'I can't imagine you not giving him hell for that.'

'I didn't want to see him. I didn't want to give him another opportunity to lie to me. He'd done that enough. He'd made a fool of me. He wasn't getting another chance.'

They'd almost arrived at his house now, but something in his brain just wasn't sitting right. Maggie Sullivan was one of the straightest-talking women he'd ever met. Just about everything she'd said was the opposite of what he might have imagined her doing.

'What part are you leaving out?'

'Nothing,' she answered quickly.

He pulled into a space outside his house and killed the engine. He turned to face her, not really wanting to say the words that were floating in his head as a possibility.

'Either you still love him, or there's something else going on.'

She made an odd little noise as air came out of her nose and mouth.

'Was that a reply?'

'That was me just hating it when you are right.'

Something washed over him. He had no right

to ply her with questions. He'd offered her somewhere to stay because she was in a bad situation, but he couldn't attach any conditions to that.

'Maggie, we've had a bad day. You don't owe me anything. You don't need to tell me anything you don't want to.'

She reached out and touched his hand. He could swear a million pulses just danced up his arm. Her fingers were warm now. They'd been cold when he'd touched her earlier.

'I don't love him. I'm not sure that I ever did. But,' she shook her head, 'we worked together in the hospital. Everyone knew. And when his wife came to the door,' she swallowed, 'she was clearly pregnant. She was so upset I thought she might go into labour on my doorstep.'

Her head was still shaking. 'This was not my story. Not my place to be. And not my issue to sort. The best thing for me to do, for myself, and for her, was to just get the hell out of New York.'

'Get the hell out of Dodge,' said Liam quietly, feeling a whole new wave of admiration for her.

'Something like that,' she said, and opened the car door. 'Thanks for this.'

He got out too and went to help with the bags. 'No problem, and don't thank me yet.'

'Why?'

'Because, remember, my house is owned by a beagle—who daycare dropped home for me a couple of hours ago, for a hefty fee.' He pulled a face. 'So, by now, he might have peed on your bed!'

Maggie threw back her head and laughed. It was just what she needed. Just what they both needed after the day they'd had.

His phone had beeped a few times while they were packing up her apartment and travelling back, but he didn't want to check it. It would be work-related. And he was finished for the day. Unless he got called directly, it could all wait.

He opened the front door to a very excited Barclay, who, of course, became even more excited to see Maggie.

Liam went to carry her cases up the stairs but she shook her head. 'Let's go straight to the laundry.'

He put the cases in the laundry room and watched as she tipped half of one case straight into the machine. 'No sorting the whites from the coloured clothes?' he asked.

'That's for amateurs.'

'Don't moan to me if all your white clothes turn a different colour,' he warned, heading through to the kitchen and pulling a couple of beers from the fridge.

He heard the machine start as she padded through. 'Oh, come on, everything gets washed at thirty degrees now…colours shouldn't run.'

He handed her a beer, which she gladly accepted. 'I have biscuits that will go with this.'

'Haven't you succumbed yet?'

'Succumbed to what?'

'To calling biscuits cookies, crisps chips and chocolate candy?'

'A cookie is a different *kind* of biscuit.' She waved her hand between them. 'You and I know that.'

'I might give you that.'

'And there's only thing that can be called chips, and it's not crisps.'

He laughed. 'I'd love to see you in a restaurant.'

'You wouldn't. Who knows what I would end up with?'

He pulled open a drawer. 'So, I do have some crisps. If you're hungry, I can make you some toast and bacon.'

'A piece and bacon sounds wonderful,' she sighed.

'A piece has an entirely different meaning in the States…'

'I get that, but I still like to say it how my granny would.'

'Grab a seat on the sofa while I make the bacon. Find us a movie to watch.'

She lifted her beer and moved to the door. 'You will make bacon for Barclay too, won't you?'

'You think I can make anything in this house without him having a bit?'

She laughed and Liam tried to still his brain while he made the food. Too much had happened today. He didn't want to have time to think. His brain would go back to all the patients he'd dealt with, and then he'd want to know their outcomes. He'd want to know if everyone was identified. He wanted to go and spend time tomorrow with Linda. If he could, he would be the one to tell her about Ben. He wanted to know about the young woman with the haemothorax, and the child with the burns.

Chances were, he wouldn't sleep a wink tonight, and neither would Maggie. This was the nature of the job.

He finished cooking, plated up the food and put some cooled rashers on a plate for Barclay.

By the time he reached his sitting room, Maggie was curled up on the sofa with *Back to the Future* playing on the TV.

'The old ones are the best,' she said.

'Absolutely,' he replied, handing her a plate.

They ate comfortably together. Arms clashing, legs touching, and once she'd finished Maggie leaned against him.

'You okay?' he prompted.

'Had better days,' she replied after a pause.

He thought for just a second, before putting an arm around her shoulders and letting her lean her head against his chest.

After a few moments, she put one of her hands there too.

He hadn't asked her, but he'd known she was

single. There had just been something about her. Almost as if she'd had an *ask no questions* banner above her.

And now he knew why. It was personal. Just over a month ago she'd been in what she thought was a long-term relationship. How long did it take to get over something like that? And why was he even wondering?

She picked the next movie too. *Terminator.* Not quite the same vibe as the previous. By the time it was halfway through she was drumming her fingers on his chest.

'I'm not going to sleep tonight,' she admitted, rubbing Barclay on the ears, since he'd joined them on the sofa. 'Even if I do have a beagle to cuddle.'

'Me neither,' he admitted. 'Brain is too full.'

She lifted her head and looked at him. 'But I don't want to go into work early, so don't even suggest it. I need some time out.'

He glanced at the clock. 'We have another seven hours.'

Her face was just inches from his. Her green eyes were still bright, even in this dim light. 'If I wasn't exhausted, I might suggest some other way to pass the time.'

No. She hadn't just said that.

Her eyes didn't leave his.

He didn't speak, but the expression on his face was clearly a question.

'Too much for today?'

He opened his mouth. Not quite sure how to respond. His body knew exactly how he wanted to respond, but parts of his brain were screaming at him.

He'd seen her almost break at one point today. She'd just told him about how she'd been treated back in New York. He'd invited her to stay here because he cared, because he was worried about her. Did she think this came with strings?

'Maggie…' he started.

'Don't,' she said as she leaned up and let her lips touch his.

Her hand moved to the side of his face as their kiss deepened. There was no doubt, no hesitation, and it felt natural. It felt as if it was meant to happen.

Barclay gave a little growl as she changed position so she was sitting astride him, and they both laughed.

'He thinks he's got a rival,' said Liam.

'He might have,' she whispered as she kissed him again.

This was so easy. So easy to get swept away and forget about all the bad parts of the world. Her scent was permeating his senses, the touch of her skin against his made every part of him feel alive. When was the last time he'd felt like this?

Short answer: never. He'd had relationships, but nothing that lasted. Liam Kelly had been on a mission for so long. Making medicine better. Ensuring people learned. Focusing only on his job. He had no time for anything else. And that made most of his potential partners walk the other way.

Or did it? If he wanted to admit it, it was usually him that ended things before anything got too serious. Relationships could hurt. And Liam had already experienced the most painful hurt in the world—losing a sibling. Why would he line himself up for any other kind of heartbreak? It was easier to walk away before anyone had expectations. Before anyone could start to plan for a future. At least that was what he always told himself.

But none had conjured up the feelings he was currently having. None had stressed his brain the way Maggie had. He almost hated her, and thought that she clearly hated him. But this? This connection? Maybe that was what this was all about?

Maybe he'd been just missing the mark for the last ten years.

She'd even conquered his dog—and that was unheard of.

'Are you sure about this?' he said, his voice so low it was almost a growl.

He didn't want to make a mistake. He didn't want to assume anything here. Maggie had surprised him on more than one occasion. And his senses were going into overdrive and overwhelming all rational thinking. So he needed to double-check.

She sat back, her eyes shining, her hands on both sides of his face. 'Oh, I'm sure,' she grinned.

He glanced downwards. 'Sorry, Barclay,' he muttered as he picked her up, and carried her towards the stairs.

CHAPTER SEVEN

MAGGIE SULLIVAN HAD lost her mind.

Things like this didn't even happen in the bad romcom movies that she'd watched.

But when she woke up the next day, with no dried, freshly laundered clothes, she realised she shouldn't have let herself get distracted.

Barclay was lying comfortably next to her with his face on the pillow, his floppy ears rumpled and his big brown eyes staring at her, as if he'd been in that position all night.

Liam was nowhere in sight.

Once she'd pulled herself together and got down the stairs, she found a note in the kitchen next to the coffee pot.

Sorry, gone back to the hospital. Come and meet me at lunch-time if you want.

So, as she dumped the laundered clothes in the dryer and flung on another load, she let the coffee pot bubble and tried to make sense of her life.

Did she regret the actions of last night? Not really. Did she wish it had happened another way? Absolutely.

She'd been offered a place to stay by a colleague when she was in a desperate situation, and after a very bad day at work.

A colleague she'd spent the last month virtually at war with.

Yes, there had been some flirting. Yes, she was attracted to him. Yes, she was pretty sure he was attracted to her. But there hadn't been the development of a normal 'relationship'.

She'd literally jumped his bones last night.

And he was gone this morning. Not hopeful.

But…the note?

Was that just…duty? Embarrassment? Something to try and placate things? Or a genuine invite?

Her brain couldn't cope with the turmoil.

Maybe she was just lousy at relationships. If the last one was anything to go by, then that was true.

And what about the fact she knew he was known as short-term-lease Liam? That was hardly encouragement to jump into bed with someone.

For a few moments, Maggie put her head in her hands. What on earth was she doing? She took a deep breath and thought about the day before. It had been horrific, and maybe going to bed together after an experience like that wasn't so catastrophic for two people who were currently single and seeking comfort.

Then her mind drifted back to Liam before they'd left the hospital last night. He'd stood up and told everyone what a good job they'd done. He'd trusted his teams to work together yesterday. She hadn't seen him second-guess anyone. Not for a moment.

There was still a chance he might want to double-check things today—but Maggie didn't think so. He'd seemed sincere last night, and she wanted to believe in him.

But what about everything else? What about the fact she was a poor judge of character when it came to guys? Had she just made another spectacular mistake? Maggie let out a long, slow breath, and tried to think clearly.

Barclay was hanging around her feet, and rubbing her bare legs with those soft-as-silk ears. It was kind of addictive.

She poured herself a coffee and walked back through to the couch, patting her legs so he would jump up and lie across her.

Her hand automatically stroked his back and it gave her a sense of calm again. This was nice. A dog, a house. Her hand stopped, and she looked around her again.

Her phone was next to her and she picked it up and did a quick search. A house like this was worth nearly a million dollars. She let out a breath. Townhouse. Four bedrooms. Garden. Good area in Chicago. It was a lot of house for one guy.

How much did she really know about Liam?

Maggie groaned and leaned her head down onto Barclay's belly.

'What am I doing?' she moaned to him, but Barclay just tried to lick her face.

So she lay there for a while.

Contemplating everything that had happened yesterday. And even though she was trying not to, she was making an automatic to-do list in her head.

She wasn't assigned to work today, but she knew she would go in—and clearly so did Liam. He'd even left the number for the doggie daycare on the counter.

But what about here…what about now?

They barely knew each other. Oh, they knew each other well enough to know that they were skilled at winding each other up, but what else?

She had to move back out. She knew that immediately. She had to find somewhere else in order to put a distance between her and Liam, and to see if anything might actually develop between them. Last night they'd finished a race that they hadn't officially started, and that didn't help anything.

She pushed away some of the intense feelings from last night. The connection. The heat. The laughter, because that had actually happened. The teasing. The feeling of fulfilment.

If she could play that night on repeat for the rest of her life, she'd be a happy girl.

But that wasn't possible.

She needed to get her life in order. She needed to be sure she was ready for this—whatever this might be.

Her heart gave a twist in her chest, and she couldn't help but smile. No one could see her. It didn't matter. She could remember the sweet parts of last night. How good things had felt. That moment when he'd wrapped her in his arms, and she'd felt his warm breath at the back of her neck and side of her cheek.

She couldn't remember feeling comfort like that.

The more she looked back on her past relationship, the more shards of glass within it she could see. Ryan had never been honest with her. He'd never planned a future with her—no matter what he said. It had all been lies.

Was she ready for anything new?

Was Liam actually looking for something, or was last night just convenience?

She gave a gulp. It certainly could have been. She'd literally handed herself to him on a plate. What if he actually didn't want her at all?

A wave of panic swept over her. Barclay raised

his nose in the air and sniffed—it was as if he could sense the change in her emotions.

She took a gulp of the coffee. Coffee that he'd invited her to drink. He'd also issued an invitation to meet at the hospital.

She dropped a kiss on Barclay's head and climbed the stairs. By the time she came out of the steaming-hot shower, Barclay was back on her bed, waiting for her.

Naked, she ran down the stairs to the dryer and pulled out some warm, fresh clothes, smiling as she pulled them on. It was the first time in weeks she was sure that nothing had a hint of stale aroma around it. She folded the rest of her clothes in a neat pile, and then flung in the next load. Her hand rested on the folded clothes and she contemplated taking them upstairs and putting them in the wardrobe in her room. She hadn't even opened it. It might already be full of things.

But it seemed presumptuous of her to do that. So, she left them on top of the dryer.

Barclay had followed her back down the stairs and his tail was wagging. She quickly phoned the daycare to book him in, then collected his lead and grabbed her bag.

The walk from Liam's house was actually pleasant. The scenery was nice. She understood why Liam sometimes chose to jog to work, and Barclay only gave her one dirty look as she dropped him off.

She hadn't packed scrubs, as she wasn't officially working, but knew she could grab some at the hospital if she needed them. Jem was the first person she ran into. She took one look at Maggie and pulled her into the relatives' room. It was clear she wanted someone to talk to.

Jem spilled everything as if Maggie was her sounding board about yesterday's events. The whole time she listened, her phone was pinging in her pocket. Maggie leaned forward and patted Jem's hands reassuringly, adding a few words. When Jem finally sat back with an apparent feeling of relief, she pointed at Maggie's pocket. 'Who is that?'

'I have no idea,' sighed Maggie. 'It did it all day yesterday, when we were at the airport. I was having landlord issues.'

She pulled her phone out and saw a screen of messages from an unknown number. She shook her head, already deciding it might be better not to read them, and opened her emails instead. Five, from the landlords' association.

She read through them and sighed. Jem leaned forward. 'Let me see.'

Maggie honestly didn't have the energy for this today. The landlord had made a counterclaim using photos that were nothing like how she'd left the apartment, along with a whole host of apparent 'neighbour' complaints about her.

She shook her head as Jem put her hand on her shoulder. 'So, did you take your own photos?'

'Of course I did. I have a whole host of photos.'

'On that phone?'

Maggie nodded.

Jem smiled. 'Then let me answer this for you.'

Maggie sighed; she felt like a failure already. Her normal demeanour would mean that her instinct would be to tear this guy apart because of his lies and bad behaviour. But she was doubting herself, about everything really.

She handed her phone over to Jem, who spent five minutes hunched over, typing furiously, and finally lifting her head with a big smile on her face.

'I sent a reply.' She smiled. 'I added the real photos. Let's see what the association says.' She looked distinctly pleased with herself.

It was the first time today Jem didn't have a wave of panic around her.

'Thank you,' Maggie said honestly. 'Let's see what I hear next.'

She stuck her head out of the room and glanced at her watch. She couldn't see Liam anywhere and lunchtime could mean anything between midday and two p.m. She decided to take the bull by the horns and headed up to the canteen. But Frank met her at the door.

'Oh, Maggie, Liam said if I see you to tell you to come to 4D.'

She blinked. It was one of the wards, but she couldn't quite remember which. 'Thanks, Frank,' she murmured and headed to the lift.

She had her security badge, even though she wasn't in uniform, so she flashed it at the nurse on the ward, and said she was looking for Liam.

'He's about to go in with Linda,' she said in a solemn voice. 'Room 223.'

Maggie headed down the corridor and saw Liam standing to the side of the door. She touched his arm and he jumped, obviously caught up in what he was about to do.

Their eyes met. She wanted to say so much. She wanted to clarify things between them. She wanted to get over this awkward moment as soon as possible.

'Hey,' was all she could say.

'Hey,' he replied and she wondered if he was just as confused as she was.

'About last night,' he started.

'Yes,' she agreed, 'about last night.' Maggie felt as if she was holding her breath, waiting for him to fill the space. Could this be any more awkward?

They both started speaking at the same time.

'Maybe this should wait until you've spoken to Linda.'

'I had a really good time.'

Maggie stood with her mouth open. It had been the last thing she'd expected him to say.

Liam looked instantly wounded. She could almost see him shrink back. So she immediately reached out her hand to his arm. She kept her voice low and gave him a smile. 'I had a good time too.'

His shoulders instantly relaxed. He held up one hand. 'But if you've changed your mind about… anything, just let me know. I realise last night might have been out of character for us both. It was a stressful day.'

She almost said it. She almost said that he was known as short-term-lease Liam, and should she just bail now? But she didn't want to. He was giving her a get-out clause. Did she want it? In the space of about two seconds, she decided not to grab it.

'It was a stressful day,' she agreed, and then gave him another smile and held out both hands, 'and you know I don't have the best judgement when it comes to men,' she tipped her head to one side, 'but, provided you know that I am still looking for somewhere else to stay, I'm willing to see where this goes.'

There was instant sparkle in his eyes and he gave a slow nod, accompanied by a smile that sent tingles down her spine. 'Then let's see how this goes,' he agreed.

They stood for a few seconds, just grinning at each other like a pair of idiots, then Liam clearly remembered why he was really there, and his face became serious.

'I need to speak to Linda.'

Maggie instantly stopped smiling. 'She doesn't know yet?'

'No. I'm going to tell her,' he said.

She shook her head. '*We're* going to tell her.'

They nodded in agreement and entered the room, Liam taking the lead.

'Hi, Linda, I'm Liam, the doctor that helped take care of you yesterday—do you remember me?'

The recognition on Linda's face was instant. She gave him a half-smile. 'Yes, yes, I do.'

'Linda,' he said gently, 'this is Maggie Sullivan—she was the other doctor taking care of you yesterday.'

Linda had an oxygen mask on her face, and was attached to a monitor. Her colour was much poorer than it had been yesterday, and Maggie dreaded to think of the true extent of her injuries. 'The Scots girl.' Linda smiled.

Maggie sat at the side of her bed, and took other hand, wondering where her family was.

Liam must have read her mind. It was clear he'd already had a chance to check Linda's notes. 'Ben and Linda were just flying home from a world cruise.'

Linda looked blank for a second, and then the memory clearly returned. 'It was wonderful. We just have to pick up Tulip.'

'Who is Tulip?' asked Maggie, feeling a stab of concern. She wasn't sure when Linda would be fit enough to pick up anything.

'Our Westie,' said Linda with a smile on her face. 'She's had a dog-sitter while we've been away. She's expecting us back…' A frown deepened her brow. 'Maybe Ben's already gone to pick her up.'

Liam shot Maggie a look and she kept quiet.

He sat on the other side of the bed and stroked Linda's hand. 'Do you remember much about yesterday?'

When Linda didn't immediately reply, he gave a prompt. 'The accident you were in?'

'Is that why I'm in hospital?' Linda asked, apparently feeling a little brighter.

She gave a cough, dry at first, then turning into something hacking. Her alarms started pinging, her oxygen rate dropping sharply, and her colour deteriorating.

Liam patted her back gently for a few moments, then let her rest against the pillows. 'I'll see you in a few minutes,' he said.

Linda closed her eyes, then opened them again, and with a weak voice asked, 'Tea, with milk please.'

Maggie already had the electronic chart in her hand and signed in to read it. It told her everything she didn't want to know. No family. Previously diagnosed terminal lung cancer with multiple metastases.

She wasn't sure if Linda also had some form of dementia, or if possible brain metastases were causing her memory failure. A scan had also revealed lots of tiny fractures throughout her body, with pain relief the only treatment at the moment.

Liam slipped his arm around her shoulders as she read, as if he could sense the tear that was running down her cheek. 'I'm going to get that tea, and then stay with her. I think she'll die soon and I'm not going to get the chance to tell her about Ben. It seems too cruel right now.'

Maggie took a breath. 'Should I go and get her dog? Bring it in to see her?'

He gave her a warm smile. 'That's such a nice thought. You'd need to clear it with the ward sister, and find out where the dog-sitter is.'

'Do you think Linda might know that? What if it was Ben that dealt with everything? Have we found any of his belongings?'

'I have no idea,' admitted Liam. 'But we could check with Leah and Anjar.'

She took a breath, walked around and squeezed his shoulder. 'Let me see what I can do.'

Nothing today had worked out the way he'd planned. He should have known better. By the time he'd reviewed the patients he wanted to and then got to Linda, he'd known he was going to stay by her side.

The fact that Maggie had almost simultaneously agreed—no need for a conversation or an argument about it—had struck him deep inside.

What was he doing with Maggie Sullivan?

Things seemed to have happened in the blink of an eye, but he wasn't sorry. What he was doing was questioning whether he was actually being fair to her.

It wasn't that Liam didn't have relationships. He did. But none of them had worked out. It was kind of hard, when he was so committed to his work.

Losing his brother from a medical mistake had shaped his whole life. There had been no guarantee that his brother's cancer would be cured—but the odds had been in his favour. The error in the administration of his chemotherapy medicines had practically shut his body down, leaving him with no defences, no ability to fight any kind of infection, and the sepsis had been almost inevitable.

It was a mistake. His family would never recover and the financial compensation hadn't done anything to help his mum and dad. A part of their joy had gone from all their lives. Of course, they still loved Liam and supported him. But every time he was around them, there was an overwhelming feeling of loss. A realization of the empty space in the room. When he'd gone to the US, they'd insisted he take the majority share of the money to buy a nice place. A place he could call home.

But what was a home without love?

He'd tried for love. But inevitably he'd always dated someone from work. And sooner or later, he'd start to nitpick. Check their work. Criticise—even though he didn't mean to. He just had that innate sense that mistakes were going to happen and he wanted to get there first.

And he couldn't stop. So, he'd tried dating women away from work. But that hadn't worked either. Because every time someone got even a little bit close, Liam felt himself pull away. And it was as if the other person knew.

On every occasion, it had caused tension and fights, with break-ups written in the stars.

And he'd started that way with Maggie too. Even though, on this occasion, he'd made a mistake.

His mother would say that Maggie was fit for him. She'd called him out almost immediately. She continued to call him out. Things felt different this time around. Could he actually have a chance of building something here?

He continued to sit with Linda. Her condition gradually deteriorated. Her breathing slowed. There would be no heroic measures to intervene in Linda's decline. It seemed she'd already prepared ahead. A Do Not Resuscitate instruction was in her notes from a few years earlier, when she'd been clear-headed.

Maggie appeared a little later, her face flushed, carrying a white ball of fluff in her arms. 'You got Tulip?' he asked.

'I got Tulip,' she said. Then whispered, 'Ask me all about it later,' as she perched on the edge of the bed.

Tulip moved immediately next to Linda's arms. She opened her eyes momentarily and gave a wide, tired smile. 'Baby,' she murmured as her hands rested on the white fur.

A few minutes later, she was gone.

Maggie sat back and swallowed. 'Wow, I didn't expect it to be quite so soon.'

Tulip made a mournful little noise and Maggie gathered her into her arms again. 'Come here, darling.'

Her pink collar was barely visible in amongst all her fur.

'Is she meant to look like that?' asked Liam. 'I've never had a Westie.'

'Me neither,' Maggie shook her head, 'and as for the dog-sitter...let's just say I wouldn't recommend them. I'm not sure how well looked-after Tulip was.'

Liam leaned forward to stroke the dog. 'What do you mean?'

Maggie sighed and dropped a kiss on Tulip's

head. 'I mean, there were lots of dogs. I think Tulip was supposed to be groomed while she was there, but…' she held out her hands '…we can both see that didn't happen.'

Liam sat back for a moment, an expression on his face she couldn't quite read. He gave Linda's hand a final squeeze. 'Let Tulip say goodbye and then we'll go. I need to talk to the ward sister.'

Maggie nodded and let Tulip have a final nuzzle with Linda before taking her outside.

Liam spoke in a low voice to the doctor on the ward and the ward sister. Linda's power of attorney was officially with her family attorney in the absence of her husband. They made a quick call to let him know what had happened, and he promised to get back in touch with the hospital staff.

Liam looked down at the bundle in Maggie's arms. 'I'm probably not going to like what you're going to tell me next.'

Maggie bit her bottom lip. 'Probably not, but I think, in the circumstances, you'll be open to negotiation.'

He sighed. 'I was going to suggest the canteen for lunch, but they don't let dogs in. Let's go somewhere across the road.'

Maggie smiled and followed him back down in the lift and across the road to a cute bakery that was dog-friendly. It was also full of the best cakes she'd ever seen.

'Skinny latte and a piece of chocolate and raspberry roulade,' she said quickly.

Liam's forehead frowned. 'How did you have time to decide that?'

She pointed. 'Spotted it as soon as we walked through the door. You should get some too. I figure you're going to need it.'

The waitress smiled as he stared over at the vast glass cabinet. He finally made a decision, 'Large black coffee, and a cream and strawberry doughnut.'

He bent down to pat Tulip, who was crouched under the table. 'She's quite a timorous little thing, isn't she?'

Maggie sighed. 'The dog-sitter won't take her back. She said she'd already had her for one extra night.'

Liam's eyes widened. 'Surely she knows they were in the plane accident?'

'Oh, she does,' said Maggie. 'Just ask me if she cares.'

'Wow,' he said, sitting back in his chair. 'You were right about me not liking this.'

Maggie dug in her pocket and pulled out a piece of folded paper.

'What's that?'

'They're the instructions that Linda and Ben sent with Tulip. Along with an enormous bag of food that I think might have been used to feed all the other dogs too.'

'Did she give it to you?'

'I *asked* for it,' Maggie insisted. 'Once I realised Linda was deteriorating, I thought it might have a bit of information on it about Tulip that we might need.'

He leaned forward and raised his eyebrows for just a second, with a half-smile on his face. 'We?'

The waitress set down their cakes and coffees, and put a bowl of water on the floor for Tulip, along with a few dry treats.

'We,' said Maggie, matter-of-factly.

Liam gave a good-natured sigh. 'So, what did we find out?'

'Tulip's age. She's seven by the way. Her feeding regime, her vet, her pet-care plan, the emergency contact—'

'Who is that?' he interrupted.

Maggie waved her hand as she lifted her fork. 'The same lawyer. I guess Linda and Ben really didn't have any family at all.'

Liam looked at her steadily as he lifted his own fork and dug into his doughnut, taking a large bite. 'I'm just waiting for you to tell me the inevitable.'

'I'm waiting for the sugar rush to hit.' Her eyes were gleaming as she said those words.

Liam took another giant bite of the doughnut. 'This is quite possibly the best thing I've ever tasted,' he admitted, then gave her a nod. 'Go for it.'

Maggie beamed at him. 'You were very gracious to let me stay at your house last night, and I fully intend to find somewhere new to rent. But,' she looked downwards, 'my circumstances have suddenly changed, and I might find it a bit more difficult to find somewhere to rent—somewhere pet-friendly, that is.'

He looked up, and couldn't help but smile at her. He could almost feel his heart swelling in his chest, because nothing he was hearing was filling him with dread. Quite the opposite, in fact.

If someone had told him a few months ago he'd welcome a work colleague into his home and consider another dog too, he would have thought them quite mad.

But sitting here today, after the events of yesterday and last night, Liam Kelly was feeling surprisingly calm.

He sat back and folded his arms, wanting a little entertainment. 'I might feel a bit contemplative about this.'

Her finger shot out. 'We're not in a workplace setting. Fancy words don't count.'

He gave her a nod. 'Granted.'

She bent down and patted Tulip again. 'Obviously, I don't know any of this. But let's just pretend that Tulip is the best-behaved dog in the world, she's completely toilet trained, and very dog friendly. Barclay will love her. For a few days at least.'

'You have to understand that Barclay is the boss of us all.'

She nodded and kept smiling. He liked that about her. Even if the odds against her were potentially huge, Maggie Sullivan would carry on regardless.

He shot a look at Tulip.

'I mean, if her staying for a few days is absolutely out of the question I can try and find a pet-friendly hotel.' She gave him her saddest possible face. 'Or, ask if she can stay at a shelter for a few days until I'm sorted.'

He held up one hand. 'You think I'm going to let a newly orphaned dog go to a shelter?'

'The dog-sitter apparently would.'

'We should check that person's references,' he replied gruffly.

'We should,' she agreed, nodding and smiling widely at him.

He looked down at the list. 'We will need to get her a dog bed, some bowls and whatever her food is.'

'I'll cover it,' she said quickly.

He rolled his eyes. 'Don't start with that.' Then he paused for a second. 'You do know there might be something in the will about Tulip? Maybe Ben and Linda made some other arrangement for her in their absence?'

Maggie bent down and pulled Tulip firmly onto her lap. 'I've only known her a few hours, but I think I can outsmart any lawyer who wants to steal my girl.'

Liam laughed, then leaned over and grabbed a bit of Maggie's roulade with his fork. She feigned shock. 'What?'

'My fee,' he said wickedly, licking the fork and nodding again. 'Nice…good choice; might try that next time.'

She took a deep breath. 'There are a few other patients I wanted to check up on.'

He nodded. 'The little girl with the burns is in Paediatric ICU. She's going to need extensive skin grafts. She was on a trip with friends, and both her parents are currently at her side. Our young woman with the shoulder injury and haemothorax had eight units of blood yesterday. She's in ICU and goes to university in Chicago; she was returning after a trip home and her sister is due to arrive today.'

Maggie let out a long, slow breath. He could tell she was grateful. 'What about the cabin crew member?'

'With the burns on her hands and arms? She's been seen by Plastics and the burns unit. Although she doesn't have a high percentage of her body burned, her injuries will be life-changing. They are already talking about a process where they grow her own skin samples in the lab to use for skin grafting.'

Maggie gave a shake of her head. 'Technology is wonderful these days. I hope it works for her.'

He gave a small shrug of his shoulders. 'Not all the patients at the scene were as lucky. They're still speculating on the news about all the causes.'

'I read the headlines on my phone on the way back with Tulip. They are going for a bird strike at the moment with catastrophic engine failure. It's lucky any of them survived.'

She looked down at Tulip. 'In the meantime, we can make sure a little dog feels loved and wanted.' She gave a brief lift of her eyebrows. 'And hopefully not bullied by Barclay.'

Liam tilted his head as he looked at her. 'Maggie Sullivan, are you ready for a dog?'

She held up Tulip, looking her in the face. 'Liam Kelly, I've never been more ready in my entire life.'

CHAPTER EIGHT

THINGS SETTLED RATHER ODDLY.

Tulip was a needy little dog, probably because she'd had two elderly owners who had spent much of their day with her.

Barclay had gone off in a huff for all of ten minutes before he'd decided he didn't mind having a companion. After one night, they shared a bed—all the beds around the house.

Maggie hadn't actually looked for another place yet. She was still receiving regular emails from the landlords' association about the ongoing issues with her landlord, who was still disputing all her claims.

Liam hadn't mentioned anything to her at all. They were living comfortably together, sleeping in the same bed at night, sometimes with two dogs. They were in some kind of relationship that neither of them had acknowledged officially.

And it was…nice. But definitely awkward.

Doggie daycare had happily taken Tulip too,

and Maggie had blinked twice at the price, which she'd paid.

Liam had said nothing when she'd moved her clothes into the cupboard in the other room, which was empty, and slid her underwear into the drawers. She knew she should offer to pay rent, but everything about that conversation felt odd.

He'd offered her a room for the night, and then said nothing else apart from that conversation at the hospital when they'd agreed to see how things went. Was she taking advantage here? Because it didn't seem like it. He made her feel welcome. He'd bought some of her favourite foods. They'd just appeared in the cupboards.

When Maggie had told him she'd need to update her address at HR, he'd just shrugged and said easily, 'Just put here.'

And so she found herself living in a beautiful house in Chicago she couldn't possibly afford, with two dogs, and one of the most handsome men she'd ever seen, wondering if this was all actually some weird kind of dream.

Underlying everything was the feeling she was missing something. Just how well did she actually know Liam? Sure, she knew what he liked to eat, what laundry detergent he used, and how affectionate he was to both of their dogs. But did she really know him?

That photo on the stairs seemed to echo around her. She'd asked if his mother and father visited, and he'd just said the flights were too long for them. She thought back to everything she'd missed regarding her ex. Was she doing the same thing again? Did Liam have a wife and family back in Ireland that she knew nothing about?

She didn't think so. In fact, she could almost take a one hundred per-cent bet on that not being the case. But the trouble was, Maggie didn't trust herself right now. Her judgement had failed her before—was it failing her again?

Liam hadn't promised her anything but to wait and see. It wasn't as though she hadn't been warned about his nickname. She just wasn't sure she wanted to be on anyone's list of ex-girlfriends who hadn't really had much of a chance, or a say in the relationship.

As nice and as awkward as things were, she would have to tackle them.

It was early. She wasn't working today and was building a shopping list in her head of what she needed to pick up. Tulip was already sitting on her chest, staring at her patiently.

The little dog had adapted well. It was almost as though she'd always been here. She had a favourite position in the kitchen and sitting room. There was even part of the hall that she liked, where the sun shone through the glass panel on the front door.

As she lay on the bed, Liam stuck his head around the door. 'Want to take the dogs out today?'

She leaned up on one elbow. 'Where?'

'Have you been to Belmont Harbour Dog Beach yet?'

She lifted her eyebrows. 'Since I've only been borrowing your dog, and I didn't have a dog of my own until a few weeks ago, that would be a no.'

She tried to sit up a little more. 'Where even is it?'

He gave her a wide smile. One that made her skin tingle. 'It's about a half-hour drive. And I know a great coffee shop and a place for lunch.'

'I'm sold,' she said, swinging her legs out of bed as Tulip started to bounce around. 'We'll be ready in fifteen.'

Once the dogs were strapped into the rear of the car, Liam took off through the streets, pointing out places along the way.

He seemed relaxed, happy. Maybe it was time to push a little further.

'How long have you been here?' she asked.

'Five years.'

'And why Chicago?'

He paused, and she could tell he was thinking about what to say. 'I wanted to get away from Ireland. I'd always wanted to try working in the States, and Chicago just appealed. I did a job in Boston first, but as soon as I came here I knew it was the place I wanted to call home.'

'Just like that?' she asked, a little in wonder.

He shot her another smile. 'Just like that. Have you never had that before? Arriving somewhere and it more or less feeling like home straight away?'

She shook her head. 'It's always been people for me that make a place like home.'

'But your family are in Scotland. Do you plan to go back?'

She stared out of the window at the passing trees. 'I'm actually not sure. In theory, maybe. My parents are gone, but I have aunts, uncles and cousins. I still love Scotland, but I don't know if I want to go back and live the rest of my life there. And I definitely like a city ER. More variety, more interesting.'

He laughed. 'If people could hear this conversation who weren't actually doctors…' He let his voice tail off and it was her turn to laugh.

'I know. We can be quite macabre.' She waved her hand, flicking her blonde hair behind her ear. 'I've seen enough drunks in Glasgow, time to move onto the next city.'

'Did Edinburgh have a better class of drunk?'

She made an exasperated noise. 'Absolutely not. They were all messy.'

It was his turn to raise his eyebrows. 'Messy? That sounds like a carefully selected word.'

She gave him a warm smile. 'Yeah, it was, but I don't need to do that with you, do I?'

It wasn't really a question. It was more the recognition. She didn't need to pretend around Liam. He knew who she was. She didn't have secrets to hide who she was.

But did she know everything about him?

'What about you? Do you have plans to go back to Ireland?'

She could see his hands slightly stiffen on the steering wheel. Most people wouldn't have noticed, but she did.

'Probably not.' His voice was quite low. 'I've visited my mum and dad a few times. And they want to come here, but it's a long flight.'

He left it there. And she wanted to push, she really did. But did she really have any right?

'Yeah, you said. Do you have more family back home?'

Her brain was fixed on that photo on the stairs, and the fact he'd never really mentioned anything about his family before.

He took a few breaths and then said rather too breezily, 'I have aunts and uncles, lots of cousins. Both sets of grandparents are dead now, but you know what Ireland's like—doesn't matter where you go, someone will always know you.'

She gave him a half-hearted smile and for a second their gazes connected. He turned back to the road and it felt as though her insides sagged. They knew he hadn't said everything. He'd chosen not to. And that made her sad.

He hadn't mentioned the brother in the picture.

It was clearly intentional. Should she just ask? She wasn't quite sure.

'Here we are.' He pointed ahead at the sign, and she watched as they pulled into a car park.

It was busy here. Lots of people milling around, and lots of dog walkers. Barclay and Tulip could clearly see the other dogs too and started barking in excitement.

They put the dogs on leads and walked down to the small, sandy fenced beach. It was clearly a safe haven for all the dog energy and as soon as they entered both Barclay and Tulip strained to get off-lead.

Both were friendly enough to other dogs, so they released them, and Liam reached out and took Maggie's hand. 'You do realise I need to shadow Barclay in case some human tries to touch him.'

She gave a nod and they walked after Barclay, who was running around the place, barking and sniffing every other dog. Tulip was a little less enthusiastic, and even though she was off-lead she trotted next to Maggie, brushing against her shin.

Liam and Maggie watched as most of the dogs played well together. One, a Bernese mountain dog, was just too excited for words, bounding everywhere and nearly squashing all humans and other dogs in its wake.

Several dogs were in the water. 'Does Barclay swim?' Maggie asked.

'It's a good question,' he said. 'I've never taken him swimming.'

He walked down to the water's edge with him and Barclay was happy to trot along, having a sniff and allowing his paws to get wet. He seemed to have no interest in going any further. Tulip looked at the water and walked away.

They kept walking around the small beach area. It was busy and there was no real place to sit down. The weather was cool, but not quite enough for them to want to stay for too long. After an hour, Liam gave Maggie a nudge. 'Ready for some coffee?'

'I'm ready for some bacon,' she said, putting her hand on her stomach. 'Let's find that café you mentioned.'

They clipped the leads back on the dogs and Liam kept his hand in hers as they strolled along, looking at a few of the cafés with outdoor tables. They came to the place he knew and both ordered coffee, toast and some bacon.

Liam was already shaking his head at her. 'How much bacon do you actually think you'll get?'

She held up one finger. 'At least one rasher. That's my minimum. Anything more than that, I'm willing to negotiate.'

She settled back in the chair, happy to watch

the boats bobbing in the harbour and all the other people walking around the area.

As the waiter set down their coffee, Liam scratched Barclay's ears. 'So, what do you think of Memorial?'

'So far?'

She gave a thoughtful nod. 'I like it. Mostly.'

He fixed her with a stare, obviously trying to work out if she was joking or not.

She pulled a face. 'Some departments are better than others.'

'Such as?'

She took a sip of her coffee. 'Radiology take too long to act on orders. It slows up diagnosis in the ER.'

Now he looked curious. 'And what would you do about it?'

'That depends,' she said. 'I haven't been here long enough to work out if this is about budget, or how the place is run.'

'What do you mean?'

The bacon and toast were set down on the table and both dogs immediately sat up.

Maggie started sorting out the food. 'I mean, does Radiology need a do-over for their systems and prioritisation criteria, or are they actually really short-staffed and the ER needs to hand over some of their budget in order to get the service we need and get our patients diagnosed quicker?'

She took a bite from a piece of toast and gave each of the dogs a rasher of bacon.

Liam reached over and grabbed the sandwich she'd just made for him, taking a large bite. 'I could give you an answer to that, but I don't want you making any enemies.'

She gave him a cheeky smile. 'I'm not scared of Radiology.'

'You should be.'

'And that could be what's wrong.'

She was drinking coffee again, thinking about how lucky she was to be here. Things could have been so different. She could still be in New York. Being lied to and deceived, without a single clue as to what was real.

He was watching her. She set down her coffee.

'You haven't asked me.'

Her skin prickled. She knew the conversation had just moved on. 'Asked you what?'

'About the photo.'

She straightened in her chair. 'Well, I did in a roundabout kind of way, and you didn't give much of an answer. So I figure you'll tell me when you're ready.'

He took another bite of his toast and she wondered if he was stalling, or if he'd already changed his mind.

'Like to get straight to the point, don't you?'

She gave a good-natured shrug. 'I call things like I see them. Always have, always will. Gets me into trouble in some places.' She dropped her voice a little. 'But hopefully not with you.'

He leaned forward, his blue eyes looking right at her. It could make some people uncomfortable. But she relished it. She liked being this close to Liam. She enjoyed the intimacy between them. The connection. It helped her understand him, and hopefully would help her understand *them*.

'So,' she said, 'are you going to tell me?'

He blinked, then looked over her shoulder for a moment. She sensed he was gathering himself, and she could give him time for that.

He took a breath. 'The photo…obviously it's me…and my brother.'

'Brother,' she repeated slowly.

He nodded. 'Ricky.'

She let the name sit there and didn't ask any questions. She wanted him to tell this his way.

'He was older than me. Two years. And he was diagnosed with acute lymphoblastic leukaemia when he was twelve.'

She nodded, but kept her mouth closed.

'Whilst it was a shock, his cancer was treatable. It wasn't necessarily a death sentence. There was a reasonable chance that his treatment would work and his cancer would be cured.'

She was trying to work out how long ago this must have been. At least twenty years or more? She knew that the odds of beating this disease had improved over time.

'And for a few years he had treatment, and things had improved. He had spells where things dipped, and then they got better.' He let out a long sigh. 'Then things just happened.'

'It puts a lot of strain on families,' she said quietly.

He nodded. 'It does, but at the time you just get through it. You live day-to-day. And with Ricky, sometimes he was really sick and Mum had to stay at the hospital with him; other times he was home in bed, and no one could visit.' He gave a sad smile. 'And he must have been totally neutropenic at times because he would just catch everything.'

He waited a few moments. 'Then, when he was fourteen, he went into hospital for his normal treatment, and never came home.' He stared down at the table. 'They killed him.'

Maggie felt a chill right through her body. The words were horrific. And delivered with such clarity.

'What?'

He shook his head and looked upwards. 'They made mistakes. A whole catalogue of errors…he got the wrong dosage of medicine and his body just shut down. He was dead within hours.'

The chill spread. Something about this story was waving red flags in her head. She felt as if she'd heard it before.

'I'm so sorry,' she whispered. Her mind was

turning over about how wrong it all was. How his brother's life had been stolen from them. Someone who may have been cured and lived a long life and still been here now. Gone, because of a mistake.

It gave her an alarming insight into Liam.

She reached over and touched his hand.

'So, now you know. Now you know that mistakes at work are hard for me. They shouldn't happen. I look to stop as many as I can. I stand over people. I check their work. I read others' prescriptions. I do it, because I know if one person had double-checked any of the ten points in my brother's care and treatment that day, they could have stopped what happened. He had so many failures that day. But if one person picks up one thing, it can mean the difference between life and death—even though they might not realise that.'

He put his other hand on his chest. 'And if I am that person, then I'm happy. I've stopped something that could have progressed. Do I care if other people are annoyed at me checking their work, at questioning something, at rereading tests results?' He held up both hands. 'Absolutely not. Because it's worth it.'

She wanted to speak. But she wasn't sure the words would come out the right way.

'I get it. I understand. You were exposed to risk failure in the worst possible way. Of course it's affected you, and of course it affects how you work.' She licked her lips. 'It's the example they use, isn't it? In the risk training that's used the world over?'

He nodded. 'It was one of the requests of our family. It took years to get them to admit liability. It took years for a proper investigation. I'd already started uni by then, training to be a doctor. I was determined to make a difference. One of the recommendations of the report was that all healthcare establishments should train staff on risk. It had been considered, but the training wasn't systematic. It was one of the main issues that was rolled out first.'

'Wow.' She sat back, regretting that one rasher of bacon she'd had, because now her stomach was churning.

Her hand went down automatically to Tulip. It was amazing the comfort a dog could give.

Liam gave her a sad smile. 'And the house. The one I own in Chicago—bought with some of the money we got.' His laugh was shallow. 'Because it doesn't matter, does it, the money? Every single person that's ever had damages awarded would always prefer if things hadn't happened. I would take Ricky standing here, every day of the week, and would happily live in a tent.'

'Of course you would,' she agreed.

Her head was swimming. The house was beautiful and she'd realised it would be out of a normal doctor's price range, but she hadn't imagined anything like this. She hadn't imagined the tragedy he'd had to go through to get here.

Her head was swirling with all this information. Did it make him resentful about his house? She hoped not. It was gorgeous, and it did seem as though he'd made it a home.

'You must miss him.' It was a simple statement and she could see the wave of hurt on his face.

He gave the tiniest shake of his head. 'I guess for some people, they aren't close to their siblings. And Ricky and I used to fight all the time. We were rivals. Until he got sick. And it was hard. Because I knew so many things that he didn't need to tell me. He still wanted us to play fight and wrestle even though he didn't have the strength for it. He wanted me to treat him exactly the same even if he was lying in bed and couldn't get a breath. He ordered me to keep going to football training, when he wasn't fit for it any more. Told me as soon as he was feeling better he'd be on the pitch and skin me.'

He bent down and picked up Barclay, putting him on his lap, and that action alone said a thousand words to her. And Barclay leaned into him. No biting, no snarling, just a dog, reading the needs of its owner like so many could do.

She gave a soft laugh at those final words. His accent had got thicker as he was speaking, as if he was recalling those conversations with his brother.

'It's odd,' he said. 'Because people that knew us before he was sick would have said we didn't really care about each other. But everything changed. I did still expect him to get better. I didn't expect him to die. It wasn't until after he was gone, I realised I'd probably had the biggest relationship I'd ever had with someone in my life. And I'd lost the person I might love the most.'

Something inside Maggie gave a little yearn. She actually felt as if she'd heard the noise out loud. She'd heard the other staff talk about Liam at work. How he occasionally dated someone, but nothing seemed to last. There was never drama, or fireworks—things just seemed to quietly come to an end. And she wondered if he ever reflected on how he felt. It seemed obvious to her. He'd suffered a painful loss before. Loving someone would mean the potential for loss again.

And what about her? She was sitting here with him now, living in his house, sleeping in his bed, and now sharing two dogs with him. Was she setting herself up for failure?

She took a breath and let herself be rational instead of emotional. At least she knew Liam did not have a history of a wife somewhere, or of cheating. She wouldn't expose herself to those possibilities again. She knew that. But would she take a chance on Liam? When he could so easily discard her like all the others?

She leaned forward and rubbed Barclay's ear,

touching Liam's hand. 'You were lucky, Liam. You have to turn things around in order to allow yourself to move forward. You had a fabulous brother. Your life may have been very different if Ricky hadn't existed. You have to look back on the good, as well as the bad, and be grateful you can remember the fun times you had together as brothers. Be glad you had someone to love like that.'

She saw a fleeting expression on his face for the briefest of seconds. She knew he was contemplating throwing that back. Lucky? How could it be lucky to have a brother who'd died because of medical negligence? But she saw him process, and knew that at some point in his life he'd done this a few times, imagining a life if Ricky had never existed. A life that would never be preferable to any family.

His face settled and he smiled down at Barclay and at her hand on his, moving so he could squeeze it with his own. 'I am eternally grateful I had a brother,' he smiled up at her now, 'even though I could give you a list of all the things he did to annoy me as only a brother can.'

She waited a moment. 'Thank you for telling me. I wasn't sure if you would.'

'You're living in my house now,' he said and held her gaze.

She wondered if this was the time. Part of her felt it wasn't—not when he'd just shared so much.

But part of her also felt that he'd just given her an opening.

'I am,' she said simply. 'But I'm not quite sure what that means. Would you like me to find somewhere else to stay?' She took a breath. 'You said you wanted to see how things would go between us, but what does that actually mean? Should I move back out and continue dating? Or does the fact we are living together actually mean something to you?'

It was the simplest question to ask, and he was used to her getting to the point. They hadn't had this conversation out loud, and if he would actually prefer that she moved on she could do that. She didn't want to be anywhere she wasn't wanted. But the truth was, Liam hadn't made her feel like that—not for a second. So she might as well ask.

He frowned at her. 'Do you want to move out?'

'No.' She didn't hesitate with her answer, and it was almost as if a few jigsaw pieces were falling into place for him.

'I know things started kind of suddenly, but I don't want you to leave. I want you to stay.'

She bit her bottom lip and asked the hardest question. 'Why?'

His face broke into a wide grin as he kept a hold of her hand. 'Because I wanted another dog and you've got one.'

She kept silent as he continued.

He threaded his fingers between hers as he held her gaze. 'Because I want to find out what we have. I still want to find out where this goes.' He took a breath. 'I'd like to see what *us* could look like. I like you, Maggie Sullivan… I like you a lot.' He frowned a bit. 'More than I ever thought I could.'

She could see that tiny flicker of recognition on his face. 'Is that a bad thing?'

He smiled and shook his head. 'I hope not. What about you? Will you stay?'

He hadn't asked her if she loved him. And he hadn't said those words about her. She wasn't sure if she was ready to say it. Not when she still didn't trust her own judgement. He'd just shared with her about his brother. It was big for him, she knew that. So that gave her some reassurance that he trusted her. Could she really take a chance again on what could be love?

She took a deep breath. She wanted to say more, but wasn't quite sure it was the right time. 'I'd like to stay; I'd like to see how this goes.' The wind blew through her hair and she gave it a shake. It was easier to resort to humour right now. Then she gave him a wink. 'But if I leave, I'm taking Barclay too. He likes me better.'

Liam laughed out loud. The mood had instantly lifted between them and her heart was feeling lighter.

He sat Barclay on the ground and stood up holding out his hand for hers again. 'There is no *way* my dog likes you better.'

'You think?' Tulip was happy, trotting alongside them as they walked around the area, which was now busy with tourists and residents.

Most of the shops were dog-friendly, so they drifted into a few and made some purchases. Maggie found a boutique chocolate store, a florist and a chic clothing store, where she hovered around the window.

'Go in,' urged Liam. 'Give me the dogs.'

'Five minutes,' she said, keeping to her timescale and coming back out wearing a brand-new bright green jacket and a pair of blue jeans.

'You don't waste time!' He smiled.

'I don't,' she agreed as she stood on her tiptoes to kiss him.

There was a shout from behind them, and one of the staff from the ER gave them a friendly wave. Maggie's eyes widened a little as she looked at Liam, wondering if he would jump back at their being caught.

But Liam seemed unperturbed and lifted his hand, shouting a hello in response.

'We'll be the talk of the steamie now!' She laughed.

'What?'

'Didn't you have steamies in Ireland? It's an old Scottish expression. The steamie was the place where women used to go to wash all the clothes—before modern washing machines.'

He laughed too. 'You surprise me every day.'

'I hope that's a good thing.'

'It is.'

'You don't mind people at work knowing that we're seeing each other?'

'I think we're doing a bit more than that.' He stopped and looked at her. 'I'm fine with people knowing that we're living together with our two dogs. I have no problem if they think I'm trying to surreptitiously win our bet by dubious means.'

She pointed her finger at him. 'Hey, we're not at work. Big words don't count here.'

He winked. 'I'm just getting in the practice.'

The warm feeling that spread through her just kept on going. It was amazing how one cards-on-the-table conversation could clear the air completely. It had given her the security that she hadn't even realised she was looking for.

Yes, they sparked off each other, but those sparks were good. And now she understood them a bit better, which would help with how she handled things from now on.

Liam hadn't hesitated to strike out on a limb for her when he knew she was in trouble. He'd reacted supportively when she'd told him about why she'd left her previous job at short notice.

Part of her didn't want him to think anything had gone wrong at work. But her pride was definitely more wounded by having had to tell him she'd been a fool over a man.

He'd been angry on her behalf. He hadn't blamed her for not realising and that had been a comfort, and made her feel less guilty.

Even though he hadn't even realised it, personally, he'd been building her confidence, and Maggie was finally starting to feel good about herself again on a personal level.

Could Chicago actually feel like home?

They stopped at a bakery to pick up some bread and some cakes. Then he drove them to a grocery store which they could take the dogs into, to get enough food to actually fill the fridge. It was odd, thought Linda, meal planning with someone. Deciding what they might make together. Finding out that he could make a killer lasagne—and telling him her speciality was chicken fajitas with broccoli, bacon and sprouts—was fun.

They loaded up the car and headed back to his house. Barclay had a little snarl or two when they got inside, obviously tired from their big day out, and quickly curled up to sleep on one of the dog beds. Tulip in the meantime perched at the front window, barking at every passer-by on the street.

Maggie hung up her new jacket in the cloakroom at the front door and took a moment to look at it there. It was the smallest thing. But it felt as if it belonged there. It felt as if she was putting down roots.

She smiled as she walked back through to the kitchen, where Liam was pulling a bottle of wine from the fridge. 'Am I worthy of the good glasses? The ones that are hidden at the back of the cupboard and look as if they have oil slicks through them?'

He laughed and pulled out the ones she was talking about. He poured the wine. 'Forgot I had these,' he murmured and then gave her a solemn look. 'As long as you realise you are directly responsible for the misbehaviour of any dogs while we drink from these.'

They clinked the glasses and headed through to the sitting room to relax on the sofa.

'Had a good day?' she asked as she rested her head on his shoulder.

She could almost hear his brain ticking. 'Best day I've had in a long time,' he admitted. 'We should keep them coming.'

Maggie looked up and clinked her glass against his again as she kissed him. 'Here, here.'

He reached down and pushed a strand of hair behind her ear. 'I'm so glad that you're here,' he said, the sincerity flowing from him. 'I've never felt like this about anyone before,' he said.

She blinked, catching her breath. She hadn't

expected him to say that. It took her by surprise, but the warmth spreading through her showed her they were the words she had wanted to hear. 'Are you sure?'

He burst out laughing. 'Maggie!' He shook his head but kept smiling at her. 'I wouldn't say it if I didn't mean it. Is it too soon? If it is, I'm sorry.'

She blinked back tears. 'No, it's not too soon. I'll take it. But if you'd told Maggie Sullivan three months ago, that this would be her life, she wouldn't have believed you.'

He gave her a cautious glance. 'So how does Maggie Sullivan feel about it now?'

She held his gaze as she talked. 'I think we can safely say that Maggie Sullivan is swept off her feet.'

'By me? But you hated me.'

She laughed this time. 'And you hated me too. But you know, we both have strong feelings.' She reached out and touched his face. 'I never guessed you could be such a sweetie. The minute I saw you with Barclay, I just knew.'

'Knew what?'

'That you weren't the grump everyone thought you were.'

'And that was good?'

Her finger trailed down his face. 'I didn't trust myself to trust anyone again. But you kind of sneaked on in there.'

He gave her a wicked grin. 'I kind of like being sneaky.'

'Then keep being sneaky, Liam, because it's made me realise you're worth staking my heart on.'

She gently tugged his face towards her, and kissed him, trying to understand how everything had just worked out so perfectly.

CHAPTER NINE

LIAM'S LIFE SEEMED to have shifted. One moment he'd been single, with one dog, and totally focused on his job. Next, he was living with someone, had two dogs, and was wondering what they would make for dinner that night.

While the sparks still flew between them, sometimes at work and at home, there was a distinct feeling of home. Of family. Of something entirely new.

People at work were talking. He'd dated colleagues at work before, but never one he'd actually worked with in his department. He knew there could be queries so he had spoken to HR, who were remarkably circumspect about things. Both he and Maggie were asked to sign disclaimers around their relationship, and HR considered the matter closed.

But that didn't stop the chatter, the smiles, the knowing looks. One surgeon had decided to deliver a witty but inappropriate remark about Maggie around Liam and had nearly been felled by Liam's ice-cold look. There were no remarks after that.

It was amazing how easy things were around Maggie. She was a remarkably tidy house guest without being obsessive. She cleaned up after herself whether she was in the kitchen or the bathroom. She kept her laundry up-to-date, folded everything and put it away immediately. She'd left a few things around. She'd put a photo in the kitchen that was of her and her parents from a few years ago, sitting on a bench with beautiful green and purple mountains in the background.

An alarming number of books had appeared in his house, and landed on the doormat on a daily basis. He might need to put up some shelves.

Tulip now had two dog beds instead of one. But, since Barclay had four, and both dogs preferred to sleep on top of each other and share, there hardly seemed any point in saying anything.

The most important thing was how Liam felt about her. He'd already told her that he'd never felt like this about anyone before her, and he hadn't. But he hadn't actually told her that he loved her, and that made Liam nervous in a way he couldn't really explain.

He'd felt strongly about a few women in the past—but not with the strength of feeling he had for Maggie. Maybe it was the way she constantly challenged him, or her tenacity, her sense of humour, or maybe it was something as simple as their Celtic backgrounds. He'd never shared his home with someone before, and he loved having Maggie around. So why did he still have that tiny sensation in the pit of his stomach that made him wonder if things might stay so perfect?

They'd both dropped the dogs at doggy daycare and arrived for a twelve-hour shift when everything started to go wrong.

One second, they were working normally. The next second, the department was in complete darkness.

It took everyone by surprise. All the staff paused, looking upwards at the lights, waiting for the emergency generator to kick in.

It didn't.

Liam immediately started shouting instructions. Candles weren't a thing in an ER, and, whilst many members of staff had a pen torch in their pocket, the amount of light that came from them was minimal.

'I need assistance!' came the shout in the dark. It was Maggie.

Liam turned on his phone to get some light and ran to the voice. She was in one of the resus rooms, where a patient had been hooked up to a ventilator. But the ventilator was plugged into one of the main points, meaning it wasn't functioning right now. She was disconnecting the machine so she could manually bag the patient.

'What do you need?' he asked, moving to her side.

'Just some light.' He shone his phone torch where she needed it while she connected the ambu bag to the endotracheal tube.

'Done,' she breathed, bagging steadily. 'What on earth is going on?'

'I have no idea. But I'll find out.'

It turned out the phones weren't working either, since they were part of a digital system in the hospital. Some electronic charts that were already on tablets could be read, but no others could be pulled from the system, or new ones created.

'First thing,' Liam said to a few staff who were near by, 'can someone run upstairs and check if this is affecting the whole hospital or just a part of it? If we know that, we know if we can safely move some patients or not. Lewis, can you and Ann stay near Maggie and take turns at bagging meantime?'

He dropped to his knees on the floor. 'These machines usually have a battery in case of power failures. It should have kicked in.'

'Just like the emergency generator should have kicked in?'

He stood back up. 'There's nothing obvious down there. Not sure what is going on—can you continue for a while?'

She nodded. 'I've got my back-up team here. I'll be fine.'

Liam heard a noise at one of the doors and saw an ambulance crew trying to move a patient and wondering why the doors hadn't automatically opened. He ran over and pushed them open, shaking his head. 'I'm sorry, guys, I have to declare Memorial closed to emergencies right now—we have no power, and no phones. Can you radio Control and let them know?'

The two paramedics looked a bit bewildered. 'No power?'

Liam held up both hands. 'Your guess is as good as mine right now. We might need you to come back and transfer some of our patients, but I hope it doesn't come to that.'

'Are you for real? We can't come in?'

'I can't treat patients in the dark.'

It was as if the guy was considering the point, then he gave a nod and pulled the gurney back towards the open ambulance.

Liam headed over to the desks, where one of the staff was on her mobile phone. 'Don't take any more patients,' he instructed. 'Tell them we're closed for now. Send any walk-ins away.'

She widened her eyes, clearly never having heard those words before. 'Okay,' she murmured.

Liam felt a hand on his shoulder. Frank. 'What do you need, boss?'

He felt a wave of relief. 'I need to find out if

the power problem can be fixed, or if we should be moving patients. Can you go to the estates office and see if anyone there can update you?'

Frank gave a nod and headed for the stairs.

Liam went back to check on Maggie. 'How're you doing?'

'Fine. But I had a child in cubicle three with a temperature. Can you check on them?'

The place remained in darkness. Frank appeared to say someone was working on the emergency generators and they should kick in soon. They were out across the hospital. One of the surgical doctors was having a meltdown because the tablet with their patient's details had run out of charge. Liam tried not to judge and handed him some paper. 'Write it down,' he said, nearly walking away.

'But how can I prescribe if the system isn't working?' he spat back.

Liam stopped. 'Write it down,' he repeated. 'Get someone to check the medicines. Both sign. Just make sure you have it recorded somewhere that can be transferred later, and make sure the notes follow the patient.'

He heard a kerfuffle coming from the waiting room and wanted to sort it out. But Maggie had asked him to check that kid. His head went one way, then the other, and he went to cubicle three, where the little boy's temperature had gone through the roof and he was starting to twitch. Liam shouted for one of the nurses to get him some rectal paracetamol as he monitored the child closely. But it was too late, and the little boy seized. Liam was calm, timing and monitoring the seizure, ensuring the child was safe and his airway maintained while talking quietly to the mum.

The nurse appeared with the medicine and he recorded a prescription so she could administer. Then they tried their best to cool the little boy down. 'Anyone know anybody in Paeds? I need a mobile number.'

One of the nurses with a friend on duty appeared, and phoned and spoke to her. She passed Liam to one of their duty doctors, who agreed to the admission, and even said they would come down and pick the child up. He was as good as his word, and appeared ten minutes later with a nurse to take the child up the stairs to Paeds with his mum.

The lights still weren't on and Liam was getting cranky. The noise from the waiting room had increased and he went to see what was going on. Patients who had already been waiting for a few hours were kicking off at being told to go to another hospital. One woman, who appeared drunk, was shouting and swearing aggressively at staff.

'Get me a glucometer,' he muttered to one of the auxiliary staff that were in the room, and when they returned, he moved over to the woman.

'That's enough from you. I'm Liam, one of the doctors, and I'm going to do a quick check on you before we ask you to leave.'

She looked indignant, but Liam pricked her finger, examined her head for any sign of injury and quickly checked her pupils. Her blood-sugar range was normal and her pupils equal and reactive. He gave a sigh. 'I was checking there wasn't a medical reason you're being so nasty to my staff, but it turns out there's not. You're just a rude drunk. It's time to leave.'

She looked as if she was about to swing a punch at him, but Frank appeared at his side and steered her to the exit door.

Frank shouted over his shoulder to Liam. 'Power cut was caused by a roads team working up the street. They drilled through the main power line…will take a few hours to fix. I'm going back down to help with the generators.'

There was another shout, and Liam headed in the direction of the noise. This was getting ridiculous.

The surgical doctor was still dealing with one patient, while another was yelling in pain, demanding morphine.

Liam went to attend to him, but saw the surgeon and one of the nurses arguing. 'Why haven't you made that up for me yet?'

The nurse was pointing at the chart and as Liam swept his phone over it, he knew exactly what was wrong. The hairs on the back of his neck stood on end.

When doctors prescribed electronically, the system carried out automatic checks. Namely around dosages. But this doctor had prescribed on paper. This surgeon was nothing to do with Liam, who had no right to check what he was doing, but the nurse was a member of his staff and she was clearly arguing with the man.

The surgeon looked up, annoyed that Liam had just shone his light on the paper chart. Liam stood next to him. 'I suggest you check your dosages.' He could hear the slight tremble in his own voice.

The surgeon was angry, and a little confused. 'Excuse me?'

Liam could feel red descend around him. 'No, I won't excuse you. My nurse is trying to bring to your attention the fact you've made a mistake.' He put his finger on the numbers on the chart. '200 mg is *ten times* the dose you should be prescribing. It should be 20 mg.'

The man's eyes widened and his head ducked down to the chart. 'But—' he started.

'Learn!' Liam spat out the word.

The doctor turned angrily to the nurse. 'You should have come back and told me.'

'I did,' she retorted, clearly angry. Her chin jutted outwards as she turned to Liam. 'Don't worry, Dr Kelly. I would never have drawn that up.' She shot a look at the doctor again. 'Some of us know what we're doing.'

It was clear the doctor was about to erupt, but Liam held up his hand in front of his face. 'Stop, and think. Go back to your risk training. Remember the case they taught you about. There were so many points at which someone could have double-checked, or someone else could have raised a word of warning. It's happened here. Be glad. You could have made a mistake that could have cost you your licence, and someone else their life.'

Liam had to walk away now. He couldn't let the rage consume him. There was too much else going on.

There was a flicker above him, then another, and finally the lights came back on.

He heard a cheer from Maggie in Resus.

He made himself walk in the direction of the main desk. 'Make sure all the systems are rebooted. Let me know when things are back to normal, and then we can start accepting admissions again.'

He checked the waiting room and saw that some people had stubbornly remained. He took a note and went to find a nurse to triage them all again, to make sure nothing was missed or not recorded.

He walked through the department. 'Take some time to transfer your paper records back to the electronic systems. Check the details, and recheck all your patients.'

He could see nodding heads, and people already starting to do the work.

Frank appeared, smeared in oil. 'What did you do?' asked Liam.

Frank shrugged. 'Leant a hand. The generator starter engine just needed a helping hand.' He walked off to wash his hands, and Liam didn't even try to hide his admiration.

He moved to where Maggie had reconnected the patient in Resus to the ventilator again, and she was already on the phone to ICU to transfer. She seemed to consider something while she was on the phone and put her hand over the receiver and whispered to Liam, 'Go and check the lifts.'

It hit him, just as it must have hit her. Oh, no. What if someone sick had been stuck in one of the hospital lifts for the last half hour? He took off at a run, calling all the lifts with the press of a button and waiting a few moments for them all to open.

The first two were empty. The third held two very bad-tempered members of staff, who were even more bad-tempered when they realised they'd come to the first floor instead of the floor they'd wanted on the upper levels. 'I'm walking,' squawked one and stomped off to the stairs, her slightly sweaty hair sticking to her face.

The second glared at Liam and thumped the

internal button on the lift again, folding her arms across her chest as the doors closed.

He heard the doors slide open to the fourth lift. There was no noise, no movement, so he assumed there was no one inside, until he heard a low groan.

His skin prickled and he moved quickly. A heavily pregnant woman was crouched on the ground in the far corner. 'Are you okay?'

She shook her head.

'Someone!' yelled Liam. 'Get me a wheelchair.'

While they waited Liam tried to persuade the woman to move. 'Tell me your name.'

'Marie McCron,' she said through clenched teeth.

'Were you heading up to Maternity?'

She nodded.

'Were they expecting you?'

Her jawline was still tight. 'Yes, but not until later.'

He gave a nod as he heard the trundle of the wheelchair behind him. 'Do you want me to take you straight up, or do you want to come back into the ER to be checked?'

Liam Kelly knew better than to argue with a pregnant woman who might be in some element of labour. Those were fights that didn't need to happen.

'I want to see my obstetrician,' she hissed.

'You got it,' he said as one of the porters wheeled a chair in, and beat a hasty retreat.

Liam helped the woman into the chair and pressed for the fourth floor. 'Who's your OB?' he asked as they ascended.

'Dr Turner,' she said, and her face relaxed for a moment.

'How far apart are those contractions?'

'You think I'm timing them?'

He tried not to smile. She'd been stuck in a lift for the last half hour and clearly been worried. He tried to remind himself she likely couldn't see her watch to time the contractions. He waited for the doors to open and wheeled her quickly down the corridor and into one of the labour ward rooms.

'Dr Kelly?' asked one of the bewildered labour nurses.

'This is Marie McCron, one of Dr Turner's patients who has been stuck in one of the lifts for the last half hour, likely in labour. Can you assess her and call Dr Turner, please?'

The nurse snapped into work mode instantly. 'Absolutely. Help me get her up on the bed, and then you can go.'

Now he did smile. He knew when he was being dismissed. He helped Marie up onto the delivery-suite bed, made sure she was settled, then left the nurse to it.

He had to check on Maggie again. They would

need to reassess the whole plan for a loss of power in the ER. It had never happened before, and the contingency had failed. They could also make improvements on how they'd handled things this time.

He hoped things had started to calm down a little since he'd left.

So when he arrived, he was struck by the calm in the place. This was good, wasn't it?

Frank stuck his head out of the main resus room and waved his now clean arm at him. Liam's heart gave a little lurch. Was something wrong with Maggie?

He got to the room and had to do a double-take. He didn't recognise the patient on the trolley straight away. Maggie was intubating and giving short, sharp instructions to staff.

Her eyes met his, and she looked away, concentrating on the patient.

'Who is this?' Liam asked, coming alongside.

'This is Leena Davis, the drunk patient who was asked to leave earlier?'

He felt his heart plummet through his chest onto the floor. 'What? What happened?'

It was as though a wave of panic was coming over him. 'She's not diabetic. And she didn't have a head injury that could have caused an altered status.'

Maggie waved her hand for the ultrasound transducer and smeared gel onto the woman's chest. The ECG leads were already showing an erratic tracing. Maggie fixed her eyes on the screen, and sucked in a breath. 'Dilated cardiomyopathy but not enough to cause the sudden issues she's having. She also vomited blood outside.'

She looked up at him. 'She's wasn't breathing. I had to intubate.'

He picked up an electronic chart and ordered the scan straight away. Something else washed over him. 'What did she come in with earlier? What was her complaint before the systems went down?'

He felt physically sick. He hadn't checked this woman's blood pressure, which could have been a key indicator that she might have had a stroke. Had she been complaining of headaches?

One of the staff nurses raised her head. 'Injury to her hand. I think she said she'd punched a wall.'

Liam's eyes went instantly to Leena's hands. Sure enough, one had grazed knuckles. 'That was it? Nothing else?'

The staff nurse shook her head. 'That was it.'

The phone rang next to them and someone else shouted. 'You can take her to the scanner.'

Maggie's hand appeared across Liam's chest. 'This is my patient. Let me take her.'

She'd intubated Leena and attached her to one of the ventilators. Liam shook his head fiercely.

'No, I discharged her… I made the mistake. I need to see this through.'

She put her face directly in front of his. 'And that's exactly why you shouldn't. Step away, Dr Kelly, and go and document your earlier decision.'

Her face was serious. He could tell she would fight with him about this, and he was surrounded by his staff. It wasn't a good look.

He stepped back. 'Okay.'

Maggie didn't say another word to him, just held on to the side of the gurney and pushed it towards the scanner.

His heart was somewhere on the floor. He'd just potentially cost someone their life. The thing he'd always vowed not to let happen on his watch had just happened, and it was all his fault.

And Maggie had seen it. He'd just lost his career and the woman he loved.

Maggie was trying to keep her professional face in place. She'd wanted to hug Liam. To tell him that everything might be fine.

The more she assessed Leena, the more she was sure this wasn't straightforward.

Once she had Leena in the scanner Maggie checked her records. She was a chronic alcoholic. Her blood levels were likely all over the place, which could have contributed to her heart rate in

Resus. Her blood pressure was through the roof. But after a few minutes the scanner showed she had no obvious brain injury. They moved from her head, further down her body. When someone was this ill, it was important they found out what was wrong.

It didn't take long to find the varices in her oesophagus and her stomach, and the cirrhosis of her liver. This woman was bleeding from everywhere. She was literally a ticking time bomb.

Maggie paged the on-call surgeon, who came to assess. He was shaking his head already. 'I can't take her to Theatre. Not with blood levels like those. Let's move her to ICU and try and transfuse her if we can. But I doubt this will work.'

Maggie took a deep breath and shook her head. She turned to one of the nurses. 'Can you see if Leena has a next of kin?'

The surgeon glanced back at her. 'I'll deal with all this. The truth is, if this woman had collapsed anywhere other than outside the ER she would be dead already.'

Maggie knew his assessment was entirely correct, but that didn't mean she had to like it. 'Thank you,' she said, as she exited the scan room and made her way back to the ER.

It took quite a while to find Liam. She finally found him in one of the store rooms, writing down equipment that needed replenishing, something that other staff members did on a regular basis.

His head shot up as she walked in. 'Is she dead?'

Maggie swallowed. The pain in his eyes was evident. It was clear he blamed himself.

'Not yet. But the likelihood is, she soon will be. She has severe liver cirrhosis and oesophageal varices which are bleeding in her oesophagus and stomach. No brain trauma, stroke, tumour or anything else. But she has a history of alcohol misuse going back twenty-five years. Her blood results are terrible. They can't take her to Theatre because she'd bleed out, her heart rate isn't stable because of her potassium levels, and the only thing they can try is to transfuse her. The surgeon is not hopeful.'

Liam slid down the wall, clutching his head in his hands. 'This is my fault. I should have picked up things earlier. If I'd been paying attention…if I'd been doing what I should—'

She cut him off. 'She came in drunk and disorderly with a hand graze. Likely, one of our nurses would have seen her, and none of these things would have been picked up. We don't run routine bloods on those who just need patching up. No one can predict when oesophageal varices will rupture. We didn't know she had those. They've never been picked up, and neither had her severe liver cirrhosis. This is a woman that didn't attend for care. She didn't have a regular physician.'

'Which is why we should have picked up on it,' said Liam, his eyes stricken with pain and blame.

She knelt down next to him and put her hand on his knee. Her phone beeped and she ignored it. 'But we don't pick these things up. Like I said, we would have patched her hand and sent her home, likely with a card for Alcoholics Anonymous in her pocket. We would have had no reason to check for any of the things she's just been diagnosed with.'

'But what if she'd complained of headaches? We might have checked her blood pressure and kept her in. What if she'd said she had a sore throat?'

'We would have looked down her throat and none of her oesophageal varices would have been seen or evident. Only a scope would show this, and there was no reason to request one.'

Liam was still shaking his head. 'I'm an arrogant fool. I picked on someone earlier who'd prescribed the wrong dose of a drug. I tore strips off him. I was too busy checking other people's work to check my own.'

'Liam, you did nothing wrong.' She was getting annoyed now. 'What was the drug dose?'

He blinked. 'What?'

'Tell me what the drug dose was.'

He told her and she could feel herself about to

erupt. 'And those are exactly the kind of things that should be picked up, and pointed out. You likely stopped a fatal error there. I hope you're going to write him up.' Maggie felt fierce now. 'You have a duty to. This is where the learning is. Not in some magical crystal ball that looks into the imaginary future of everyone for what might be. It's in the direct things, the mistakes we *do* make, and we *can* correct.'

'And you don't think there's something to correct in what I did?' She could hear the anguish in his voice. But she wasn't going to buy into something she didn't believe in. Because she was Maggie Sullivan, and no matter how much she loved Liam Kelly, she wouldn't let him beat himself up with guilt that wasn't deserved.

'Liam, let me be frank with you. If I thought you had made a mistake here, I would tell you. There was nothing in her presentation that could predict this woman's future. We were in a crisis situation. We had no lights, no phones and some equipment that wasn't working. The patients sent away were directed to other care centres. She was rude and drunk. You checked her blood sugar in case she was actually diabetic—which she wasn't. You checked her pupils and her head to make sure she had no sign of a head injury that could have led to altered behaviour. Have you gone back in and seen what her blood alcohol level was? It was through the roof, but the sad thing is, that's probably normal for her.' She took a breath, trying to calm herself down. 'If I could have waved a magic wand, and told you that this woman had varices about to erupt, major cirrhosis of the liver and cardiac damage—do I think we could save her?' She shook her head. 'Because the other sad thing here is that I don't think we could. I think her chronic alcohol problems have wreaked too much havoc on her body, and there would be no options left for her. Terribly sad, of course it is, but we have to face facts. We can't save everyone. Even when we want to.'

He still looked shattered. She knew he was processing. She knew he was still blaming himself, and she just wasn't sure she could do anything about it. She was failing him. She was failing the man she loved.

He looked up and there was a blankness in his expression. 'I need to step back. I need to take some time.'

'What do you mean?'

It was as if something had just flipped in his head. 'This,' he said with a wave of his hand. 'Us… I've got too comfortable. It's made me complacent at work. I need to take a step away. I need to get back to where I was. Someone who doesn't make mistakes. I can't live like this. I can't let this happen.'

Maggie felt as if her brain had just gone into freefall. 'What on earth are you talking about?'

'This…us. I'm not thinking clearly.'

She touched his arm, and tried to quell the fury that was rising inside her. 'This is nothing to do with us. You haven't made a mistake because of us.' Her voice was rising and starting to shake. 'You haven't even made a mistake, Liam, if you'd actually take the time to consider things. And if you had,' she paused and looked at him, 'it would be because you are human. Because, right or wrong, human beings make mistakes.'

He looked at her in horror, and she started questioning everything in her head.

'Someone could be dead—probably will be—because of something I should have picked up on. I have likely destroyed some family's life.' The words were hissed and the expression on his face made her step back.

She held up her hand. 'Stop. Stop this right now. This woman has a long history of alcohol abuse. Abuse which has destroyed her body, and led to all of the issues today. Her family have likely tried to intervene on multiple occasions without success. Will they be upset? Of course. Will they blame you? Absolutely not because there's no reason to.'

But Liam just kept shaking his head. Maggie felt as if she'd just stepped into a bad dream. Her defence mechanisms started to kick into place. She could pick all this apart, but Liam clearly wasn't listening. It was easier to blame her, blame them, over a perceived mistake that he couldn't process.

But that was no use to her, and no use to him. Most of all, it was no use to them.

She'd been warned. She'd had a fair chance to protect her heart from everything around Liam Kelly. Short-term-lease Liam was named that way for a reason. And she had been a fool.

She'd already wondered about their relationship on so many occasions. But her heart had overruled her head. And now, the first time that the chips had been down for the two of them, he'd pushed her away.

Two heartbreaks in one year were two too many.

'No. You don't get to push me away.'

'I'm sorry?'

'You should be, because from what I've heard, this is what you do. You reach a stage in a relationship, then you push your partner away.'

His brow furrowed. 'No, I don't.'

'So you don't know your nickname is short-term-lease Liam?'

'What? I don't even know what that means,' he said dismissively.

'Well, you should. Because that's what the staff call you.'

'That's rubbish.'

'Ask any of them. They all say it, but you know what, Liam? You don't get to do that to me.' She leaned forward and poked a finger against his chest. 'Because guess what? I get you, Liam. I get why you're the way that you are, even if you don't.'

He looked exasperated, and he'd taken on that arrogant air that he'd first had with her. 'Really? Then tell me what I am.'

She stopped for a minute, letting her brain clear. She loved this man. She didn't need to hurt him.

She spoke slowly and in a low voice Said, 'You were hurt, Liam…as a teenage boy you lost a family member you loved—probably your most important relationship at that point—and all you can remember is the hurt. And you never learned to deal with it. You never allowed yourself to move past it, and because of that you won't allow yourself to be in that position again. You won't allow yourself to really love someone, in case they hurt you. I get that. I do. But you're an adult now, an adult who has lived a life and been exposed to a world of hurt, both yours and other people's. You're better equipped to deal with it now. You have the tools to deal with life. You just have to believe you can do this. You have to learn to open up yourself, really open yourself to what's out there.' She realised she must sound pleading now, and she really didn't want to. But she kept going.

'It's about risk and you've always known that. And it's not just risk at work, it's the risk of your heart, of letting yourself love, and be loved, and taking a chance on love.'

There was no flicker of recognition or emotion behind his eyes. It was as if she were talking to a brick wall.

'You can keep going as you are, and end up a lonely old man—maybe even with a hundred dogs. Or you can put yourself out there, and let yourself be loved, knowing that one day you might get hurt.' She shook her head fiercely. 'But I'm not doing that, I'm not doing that now, or in the future.'

There was silence for a few moments and her heart gave a little burst of hope that she'd got through to him, that he'd listened. She knew Liam liked to process things, and it had been a huge day. Everything was hitting him all at once. She could only hope that his heart would win through.

But his expression hadn't changed.

Instead, she let the fury from deep inside her stomach build and flood over her. Most people thought Maggie's fury would be tempestuous and full of outbursts. Very few people knew that Maggie's most dangerous fury was icy cold.

'You want time? You want space? You can have it. Put me on alternative shifts to yours. I'll move out tonight. Tulip and I will be out of your hair. You want to be on your own? Then let me give you exactly what you want, and exactly what you deserve.’

And Maggie turned, and walked away.

CHAPTER TEN

HIS HOUSE DIDN'T used to echo like this.

It had been a week. And Liam felt as if his heart had been ripped clean out of his chest.

By the time he'd got home from work, still as confused as ever, Maggie had cleared out her things, and Tulip was packed up too.

Barclay had been whimpering, and also looking at him as if he was the stupidest human on the planet. Which he might actually be.

Frank had had a quiet word in his ear, telling Liam he was making a mistake and to rethink everything before it was too late.

Maggie was still working in the ER. He'd changed the rota as she'd asked so she worked opposite shifts.

His head was still trying to make sense of things.

At first he'd been indignant. He didn't push people away at a certain point.

Until the obviousness and clarity had become apparent. He could write down the details of every relationship. He could sense when he'd first been happy, then wanted to run. It was never for a good or rational reason. Likely because he hadn't understood it himself. And he'd always been polite, courteous, and amenable to taking responsibility for breaking things up and not being able to commit.

But he hadn't reached that stage with Maggie. He hadn't got there with her. And the red flags she'd waved to him seemed like a magic semaphore.

How could other people see in him what he couldn't see in himself?

Maybe he should find a therapist. Americans were big on therapists, but Liam had never really liked talking to people, and he particularly didn't like talking about himself, so it didn't feel like a good fit.

He'd gone over and over in his head all the things that had gone wrong with the patient—Leena. He tried to imagine how he would have reacted if another doctor had looked after her.

Would he have been rational and reviewed all the documents and test results? He wasn't sure that he would. But when he picked it apart, and tried to reassess it independently, he wasn't sure if her outcome would have been different if she'd presented on a normal day.

There had been no obvious sign of her impending events. Maggie had been right. It was likely a nurse would have asked her a few questions, patched up her hand, and sent her on her way. There was always a chance that a particular question could have led to more questions, a different consideration or test, but he couldn't possibly know that, or guarantee it.

He'd asked the senior clinician in the hospital to review his actions. He'd read the case, reviewed the notes and shaken his head. 'Why are you even asking me to review this? You did nothing wrong. This outcome could not have been predicted with the information available at that time.'

It made Liam question himself even more. It made him question his attitude to risk. Was he doing more harm than good? The other event that day would have been picked up if the electronic prescribing had been working. It had already been picked up by the nurse who'd been questioning the other doctor—there hadn't really been any real reason for him to get involved, but he had. Was it because he was always looking for failure, instead of believing in the abilities of the people around him?

The sad fact was that people—humans—did on occasion make mistakes. No one was infallible, including him. Something that Maggie had tried to point out to him. Something that had horrified him on that day at the time.

Maybe it was time for him to take a step back, get some feedback, and look at risk again.

He walked down his stairway and stared at the picture in the hall. Ricky had still been a teenager when he'd died. He hadn't been a fully formed adult. But in Liam's head, Ricky had grown with him. At times, he did imagine things his brother might say to him at various points in his life. Most of them weren't complimentary, but they were things that only a brother could say.

He sighed and moved into the sitting room. Pulling out his phone, he stared at it for a bit, as if he could wish things to happen.

Eventually he dialled. It was only a few rings before the phone was answered. 'Hi, Mum.'

'Hi, honey, how are you? It's so good to hear from you.'

There was that instant spirit lift and recognition of his mother's warm tone.

'I met someone,' he said abruptly.

'Oh?' His mother said it like a question with a rise in her voice.

He let out a breath. 'But I think I've messed things up.'

'Tell me,' said his mother, like a woman with all the time in the world.

So he did.

Maggie wasn't quite sure what she wanted to do now.

What she was absolutely, definitely sure of was that she didn't want to cry any more.

Lisa, one of the nurses, had let her and Tulip bunk with her. But Maggie had made appointments to view three apartments in the next week. She'd finally heard back from the landlord's associated and they'd found in her favour, so at least she didn't have a black mark against her name. She didn't want to take advantage of Lisa's good nature and outstay her welcome.

Work had been fine. Everyone knew they'd fought. Most people were sympathetic, but Maggie hadn't involved herself in any conversations about the break-up. It was no one's business but theirs. The only person who'd made a comment was Frank.

'Liam's a man who's had trauma in his life. I don't know the details, but I recognise the signs. You might need to give him some leeway.' They had been his first, and last, words on the subject, and Maggie hadn't responded. Because she knew he was right.

Her first sign that something was wrong was when she walked in for her night shift and everyone looked at her.

'What?' She glanced down at her scrubs. 'Have I spilled something?'

'Someone needs to see you,' Jem said. 'It's about one of the patients we dealt with at the aeroplane crash.'

Maggie gave a nod. 'Where are they?'

'Office, bottom of the hall.'

It was a little unusual but she didn't think much of it. She gave a few knocks at the door and walked in.

Then stopped. Liam was in the room too, and a woman was sitting at the desk. She'd obviously been crying, since there was a pile of tissues on her lap.

Liam looked up. 'Mary, this is Maggie Sullivan, the other doctor I was telling you about.'

Mary moved like a whirlwind, crossing the room and sweeping Maggie up in a giant hug. 'Oh, thank you. Thank you so much. I'm so sorry, but like I said to Dr Kelly, I should have come here sooner. My daughter, Jess, is so much better because of you. Do you want to see a picture?'

Maggie didn't even have a chance to reply before Mary pulled out her phone and scrolled to a photo. If she'd been worried about placing whoever Jess was, it all came back to her in an instant. This time she was looking at the pale, smiling face of the young woman she'd helped pull out of the twisted plane structure. The one into whom Liam had inserted the chest drain, and who'd been transferred to ICU. Maggie hadn't even known her true identity.

The tension that she'd felt from being in the same room as Liam disappeared. 'Oh, she looks so much better. Can you tell her that I'm asking for her? If she's well enough now, I'll go up and visit.'

'She remembers your accent.' Mary beamed. 'She said a Scottish angel talked to her while she was unconscious.'

Maggie blushed. 'Well, I'm definitely not an angel, but I did talk to her before we moved her. I'm just so glad to hear she's doing so well. Do you have any questions for me?'

'Oh, no.' Mary shook her head and pointed at Liam. 'Dr Kelly's been so kind. He's talked me through everything. He's been so patient with me. When I said I had to wait to meet you, he insisted on staying with me.'

'Did he?' said Maggie, glancing over her shoulder at Liam's face.

Mary glanced at her watch. 'Oh, I'm so sorry, I've been here for so long. Thank you both so much for your time. I should get back to Jess.' She rushed over to the table, collected her tissues, gave Liam a hug, Maggie a kiss on the cheek and swept out of the room like a tornado.

Maggie waited until the door was closed. 'How long was she here?' she asked in a low voice.

'Three hours,' replied Liam, waiting for her to turn around again.

Maggie nodded and spun around. 'Was she like that for the whole three hours?'

'Absolutely.'

Maggie smiled. 'Good.'

She was ready to go now. She could be civil to

Liam at work but she didn't want to play at being friends. Her hand was on the door handle already.

'Maggie, please wait.'

His voice sounded hesitant.

She paused, her heart already thumping in her chest. 'Is this work, or not? Because I don't want to get into anything personal at work.' She closed her eyes for a second. 'Because in case you haven't noticed, I don't seem to be very good at that.'

There was a pause, and then a warm hand on her shoulder. His voice was deep. 'I think we both know who is bad at things.'

She took a moment and then turned around.

Liam looked tired, as if he hadn't slept all week. There were dark circles lurking under his eyes, lines across his forehead and at the edges of his eyes.

His hand stayed on her shoulder. He was close, facing her. When she looked up, she could see the rise and fall of his chest. It brought back memories of falling asleep on that chest.

'I miss you,' he said. '*We* miss you. Both of you. I hadn't even considered any of the things you said to me before you said them.'

She gave him a sad smile. 'I realised that.'

He took a deep breath. 'I spoke to my mum.'

She looked up into his eyes. She'd been avoiding this, because every time she looked into these blue eyes she was lost. 'What did your mum say?'

'I told her all about you. I told her what I did.'

Maggie wasn't sure whether to be glad, or whether some irate Irish mother might want to give her a piece of her mind about speaking frankly to her son.

'And?' she prompted.

He gave a small laugh. 'Oh, she's your biggest fan. Told me I should have met you years ago.'

Her heart gave a hopeful pang. 'And what about you?'

He put a hand to his chest. 'Me? I'm a fool. A fool who is terrified to love someone in case I lose them.' His eyes were sincere. 'It seems you do know me better than I know myself.'

She wanted to breathe a huge sigh of relief. But they weren't there yet.

She decided to take a risk. 'I told you that because I love you, Liam…words I didn't have the courage to say out loud because of my last experience. And I want you to love me back. I want you to decide I'm enough to take a risk on—because we could break each other's heart at some point. But I need you to be all in, just like I am.' She could feel her heart twisting in her chest as she said the words, because now she wasn't angry with him, she was just incredibly sad, and maybe even a tiny bit hopeful.

He nodded slowly. 'You're not like anyone else I've known, Maggie Sullivan.'

'I hope not,' she agreed.

He reached and touched the side of her face with a feather-like stroke. 'I love you. I love you with my whole heart. And I won't pretend I'm not terrified you'll decide I'm not enough for you, and want to leave in a while. But in the meantime, I want to hang on in there, holding on with both hands, and both leads, and hope you'll decide to take a chance on me, and Chicago, and decide to stay a while longer.' She could see in his blue eyes that he meant every word.

She took a breath and blinked back some tears. 'What about the risks?' She smiled. She had to be sure. She had to be oh, so sure.

He shook his head and smiled too. 'I'm going to do some re-evaluating. I will make a mistake at some point. Maybe I did already, and don't even know it. While I want my workplace to be as safe as possible, I need to learn how to manage my fear about risks too.'

She moved forward, resting both hands on his chest, and then sliding them up around his neck. Her heart was slowly unclenching in her chest. She had to trust herself to be able to take a chance again. If Liam could reach out, so could she.

'Tulip doesn't like being a single dog any more. She's learned that she's part of a pair.'

His arms fastened around her waist. 'Part of a pair. That sounds good.' He dropped a kiss on her cheek. 'What would it take to persuade you to be part of a pair too?'

She stood on her tiptoes and whispered in his ear, something for him only.

His eyes gleamed. 'Let's see about making that happen.'

They left the room to a cheer from the surrounding staff that made them both jump.

'Thank goodness!' someone shouted.

'Did I win the bet?' asked another.

'What bet?' Maggie asked.

'The word thing. I bet that you would win. Did you? Is it over?'

Liam's smile was the broadest she'd ever seen. 'Did we give up on the word thing?' He glanced down at her 'We could keep that going for another year. Maybe even a lifetime?'

There was a whole host of groans all around.

Liam held up one hand. 'How about if we call it a draw? We'll both bring doughnuts.' He whispered in her ear, 'We could even call it our engagement party.'

'That would require chocolate cream aragostines, from a very special Italian coffee shop.'

'I think I can do that,' he said, 'because I'm all in.'

'Then so am I.' She smiled, and kissed him.

* * * * *

If you enjoyed this story, check out these other great reads from Scarlet Wilson

Hawaiian Kiss with the Brooding Doc
Nurse's Dubai Temptation
Melting Dr. Grumpy's Frozen Heart
Her Summer with the Brooding Vet

All available now!